MURDER
in the
EAST
ROOM

MURDER
in the
EAST
ROOM

Elliott Roosevelt

St. Martin's Press • New York

Production Editor: David Stanford Burr

Library of Congress Cataloging-in-Publication Data

Roosevelt, Elliott, 1910–1990.
    Murder in the East Room : an Eleanor Roosevelt mystery / Elliott
Roosevelt
        p. cm.
    "A Thomas Dunne book."
    ISBN 0-312-09878-2 (hardcover)
    1. Roosevelt, Eleanor, 1884–1962—Fiction.   2. Women detectives—
Washington (D.C.)—Fiction.   3. Presidents' wives—United States—Fiction.
4. Washington (D.C.)—Fiction. I. Title.
PS3535.O549M848   1993
813'.54—dc20   93-26590
                                                     CIP

First Edition: November 1993

10 9 8 7 6 5 4 3 2 1

To my wonderful children
(all eight of them),
and, as always, to my wife, Patty

I

In 1932, when her husband ran for President of the United States, and in 1933, when they moved into the White House, the world had seemed a threatening place. People had been hungry. People had been angry. It had not been altogether certain that the American system could survive.

That had been her husband's first priority: to see the American way of life survive and become vital again and prosper. Or maybe that had been his second priority, since his first had really been to relieve human suffering. Now, in 1940, human suffering in America had been relieved. Not everything her husband had done had been a success, but those who were angry now were angry for a different reason: that Franklin D. Roosevelt had changed the political philosophy of the government of the United States, had changed it, in his own terms, to a more humane government, had changed it, in some others' terms, to a socialist government.

Even so, the naked hatreds of the 1936 campaign were of the past. If they persisted in many minds, they had been shoved to the rear. Even the most rabid Roosevelt-hater's attention was distracted by what was happening in Europe

1

and Asia. The world was again a threatening place, even more threatening. The very survival of Western Civilization was at stake.

Yesterday the news had been grim. Though the great majority of Americans did not understand the significance of it, the news had been extremely grim. Mrs. Roosevelt had been puzzled at first, then distressed, to hear how many Americans could smile and be happy about the evacuation of the British Expeditionary Force from Dunkirk. Most of those who were happy were Anglophiles. They deceived themselves into believing that a disastrous, costly retreat, followed by an ignominious evacuation—however heroic— was good news. Others, Anglophobes, rejoiced in the British catastrophe. Interviewed on the Blue Network, one "man on the street" said he'd "rather be found in bed with a Jap than a Brit." Some Irishmen exulted in a British defeat, no matter at whose hands.

The Allies were in headlong retreat out of Belgium and northern France. Great Britain had changed governments. The new Prime Minister, since May 10, was a sixty-five-year-old man named Winston Churchill—in whom she, Mrs. Roosevelt, could have little confidence, remembering him as the author of the Gallipoli disaster in the last war and in the decades since as an unreconstructed British imperialist, opposed to such fundamentally just concessions as freedom for India. The French government was apparently bewildered. People were fleeing Paris. It seemed the Germans might achieve in a few weeks what they had failed to achieve in four bloody years, 1914–1918.

The hateful German dictator was allied to the Italian dictator and the Russian dictator, also to the Japanese militarists. Except in small enclaves like Switzerland and Sweden, democracy was dead from the Pacific Ocean to the English Channel. Except as a cherished memory, the values of Western Civilization were dead over the same expanse of land and to the hundreds of millions of people who lived there. If France fell, it was difficult to see how Great Britain would survive. If Great Britain fell, it was difficult to see how the United States could save democracy and Western Civilization.

Perhaps the most distressing aspect of the crisis was the way Americans persisted in ignoring it. A Gallup Poll published just last Saturday showed that only fifty percent of the American people favored drafting men into their country's service—in spite of the conspicuously growing menace. Americans were more interested in the baseball season. Great crowds continued to flock to the World's Fair in New York. A flagpole sitter trying for a new "record" had received more front-page newspaper space than the fall of Eben Emael, the great Belgian fort that had been expected to slow the German advance for weeks, if not actually to stop it.

(A cartoon in *The Saturday Evening Post* showed a smiling, squinting, speculating Uncle Sam looking into his closet, where hung a gaudy bemedaled uniform with a sash lettered: GRAND EXALTED SAVIOR OF THE UNIVERSE. A motherly woman was saying, "Oh no, Sam, not again!")

The world crisis had raised a disturbing personal question, too. The President was receiving thousands of letters daily, hundreds of telegrams, and scores of telephone calls from every kind of people, from the most humble to senators and governors, urging him to do what until then had been unthinkable: run for a third term as President of the United States.

He didn't want to run. Mrs. Roosevelt knew he was sincere about that, was not just playing coy. He was tired. He was more than tired; he was exhausted, and he genuinely looked forward to retiring to his home on Crum Elbow, commonly known as Hyde Park, relaxing, and setting to work to write his memoirs. He would be fifty-nine years old on January 30, 1941; and he, more than other men, had reason to be tired. He dragged a crippled body around, with more strain and agony than anyone not very close to him could possibly imagine. He needed rest, and the time had long since passed when the President of the United States could really rest.

This day was an example. This day, apart from everything else he had to think about, he had anxiously received every word from London and Paris. The evacuation had been successful. Most of the men of the B.E.F. had been brought back across the Channel—absent, though, most of their equipment. (Mental note: "We've got to send them all we can: guns, ammunition . . .") The armored units the Germans called panzer divisions were turning south once more, and their objective was obviously Paris. (Mental note: "Is there *anything* we can do to shore up the French defense?") Calls from the Capitol: help the French and British, *don't* help the French and British; *do* whatever is necessary to save Western Civilization, *don't* get our country suckered into war again the way we were in 1917; *ask* for a selective service act, *don't* ask our boys to throw away their lives to save corrupt old European countries; *send* arms, *don't* send anything until the Europeans pay their debts from World War I.

At this hour the President was doing something of which Mrs. Roosevelt had never been able entirely to approve. He was in the West Sitting Hall, which served presidential families as a sort of living room for the private quarters; and he was enjoying his early-evening ritual of shaking martinis and sharing them with his closest friends. He had done it in Albany when he was Governor, in spite of Prohibition. He had done it in the White House before Repeal as well as after. He was doing it tonight, in spite of the fact that shortly he had to dress and play host to a formal dinner.

The cocktail hour would be abbreviated this evening. He had asked only two friends to join him: his personal secretary Missy LeHand and his assistant and confidant Harry Hopkins.

Passing through the West Sitting Hall on her way to her rooms to dress for the dinner, Mrs. Roosevelt smiled and greeted Missy and Harry and did not remind the President that he must be ready by 7:30. If he had forgotten it, Missy had not. Missy accepted responsibility for a great many things and happily relieved the First Lady of some onerous burdens.

"Damned nice of Jim Farley," said Missy to the President. She referred to the fact that the President's former campaign manager and postmaster general had announced his own candidacy for the Democratic nomination in 1940. "With friends like him—"

"Politics, Missy," laughed the President. He slapped her lightly on the leg. "An ambitious man. And why shouldn't Jim be ambitious? The fact that he hasn't the chance of a snowball in hell doesn't seem to occur to him, and that's what I hold against him. The party will not nominate another New Yorker immediately, and the country won't elect one."

"Not Dewey?" Hopkins asked wryly.

"Well now, the Republicans might nominate him," said the President. "But the country won't go for him."

"Give me the best reason why the country won't," said Missy.

The President laughed. "He's too cute!"

The orchestra in the State Dining Room—a group from the Marine band, in dress uniform—struck up "Ruffles and Flourishes." The guests, the men in white tie, the ladies in gowns, rose to their feet. The orchestra continued into "Hail to the Chief," and the President entered the room, wheeled by his valet Arthur Prettyman and flanked by the First

Lady, who was wearing a tea-colored silk gown decorated with lace.

At the head table, Arthur helped him to transfer to a dining chair, which task he finished about the time the orchestra reached the end of the music.

"Ladies and gentlemen, the President of the United States!"

The President lifted a glass of champagne and said, "The United States!"

He sipped from his glass, then shoved it disdainfully aside. As always, White House champagne was cheap New York sparkling wine, barely palatable, scorned by every guest, yet served because Mrs. Roosevelt, hostess of the White House, could see no reason to tax the budget, which was spare enough at best, with expensive French wines—and besides she was hardly aware of the difference.

Officially, the dinner was nonpolitical, arranged to honor members of Congress who had announced they were not running for reelection in 1940, and the guests included both Democrats and Republicans. Besides the retiring congressmen, a number of prominent members who would remain were guests, as were a few leading political figures of both parties.

Seated to the President's left was Alfred M. Landon, the Republican he had so decisively defeated in 1936. To his right was the brilliant lyric soprano Lily Pons, who would sing in the East Room after the dinner. The President, somewhat like a fan at a tennis match, turned his head right to left and left to right, to speak to Governor Landon, then to Miss Pons, then to Landon again, and so on.

Another Republican seated to the left of Mrs. Roosevelt, was Henry Stimson, whose political affiliations went back to Theodore Roosevelt.

"In some ways, Mr. President, I am glad you won in 1936," said Landon. "I should not want to face the responsibilities you face in 1940."

"I daresay you would face them courageously, Governor," said the President. "A man faces what he has to."

Mrs. Roosevelt enjoyed conversation with Henry Stimson. Fellow New Yorkers, they had known each other for a very long time. Stimson had been Herbert Hoover's Secretary of State. Of late he had become a spokesman for preparedness.

"I believe, Mr. Stimson, you are to give the commencement address at Yale University this year."

"Yes," said Stimson. "I have that honor."

"I can think of no more distinguished speaker they might have," she said.

Stimson accepted the compliment with a graceful nod. He was a tall, spare man of seventy-three, with thick gray hair and a neatly trimmed mustache. His long face was still the picture of strength it had always been.

"Will you speak again on preparedness?" the First Lady asked. "If I am not asking you to disclose a confidence . . ."

"Yes, definitely," said Stimson. "What I say will depend very much on how the battle in France develops between now and the date of the speech. One thing I intend to say is that our country is appallingly unready for a major war, so the only thing that stands between us and Hitlerism, should France fall, is the British fleet. If we do not sustain the British nation, with everything we can send them, we stand in peril of losing our freedom."

"I agree with you," said Mrs. Roosevelt.

"We must repeal that shabby piece of cowardly insanity, the Neutrality Act."

"That will be difficult . . . politically."

"We must initiate a peacetime draft."

"More difficult," said Mrs. Roosevelt quietly.

"Many Republicans are ready to read me out of the party," said Stimson gravely.

"Isolationists," said she.

He nodded. "Isolationists, yes. Of course—" He paused

and smiled. "Of course the *progressive* wing of the party, and its right wing, are at bitter odds."

"Who will they run for President this year, do you think?" she asked.

Stimson shrugged. "The most able man in the Republican Party is Senator Robert Taft. He is a fellow Yale man. Unfortunately, he focuses his singular intelligence and ability on a conservative course—which I am afraid includes a strong disinclination to involve this country in taking up the British cause."

"And what about Thomas E. Dewey?"

"Oh, Tom's all right, as far as he goes. But he doesn't seem to go much further than dapper and mellifluous."

Mrs. Roosevelt laughed. "Mr. Stimson!"

"I will say one thing for either man, Taft or Dewey. It will take a strong candidate to beat one of them. Also, don't discount this man Wendell Willkie. He's no isolationist. He'll be a tough campaigner."

"The Democratic candidate will have to be a tough campaigner," said Mrs. Roosevelt.

"And who do you think that might be?" asked Stimson.

"I know the President has three men in mind. Secretary of State Cordell Hull, Secretary of Agriculture Henry Wallace, and Harry Hopkins."

"Does he not have a fourth man in mind?"

"Perhaps. Of whom are you thinking, Mr. Stimson?"

"Himself."

Mrs. Roosevelt shook her head. "I think not," she said. "I *hope* not."

"I know the burden is great," said Stimson. "I know the tradition against a third term is all but insuperable. But remember another tradition: that no President has ever retired in the face of a crisis."

"I speak to you in confidence, Mr. Stimson. I know I *can.* The doctors pronounce the President's health better than it has been in years. But there is a certain weakness, you know. He is tired, Mr. Stimson. He is very tired. It is the sort of chronic weariness a long vacation cannot cure—even if he could take a long vacation."

"I speak to you in confidence also. I am a lifelong Republican, as you know—"

"Uncle Ted spoke very warmly of you," she interrupted.

"I was honored to be able to serve Theodore Roosevelt. But—I was saying, I am a Republican, and for me to urge the President to run for a third term is heresy. If it became known that I did, I'd be drummed out of the party. Nevertheless, I should appreciate your telling your husband I hope he will run. It will be an immense personal sacrifice. But the crisis is so great—"

"I will tell him what you said, Mr. Stimson."

They had dominated each other's attention for several minutes, and courtesy required that Mrs. Roosevelt and Henry Stimson turn and speak to other people. For Mrs. Roosevelt that meant speaking to Cordell Hull. The Secretary of State was a warm and gracious man, a pleasure to talk to. But he was distracted, and they talked only for a minute. Mrs. Roosevelt was left with time to look around the room, smiling and nodding at some of the guests.

She noticed that the Vice President, Cactus Jack Garner, sat at a different table from Congressman Sam Rayburn. At Rayburn's table was a young man noted as a promising new politician: Congressman Lyndon Johnson. The story around town was that Rayburn treated Johnson like a son and Johnson treated Rayburn like a father.

Senator Truman was there. Mrs. Roosevelt did not see his wife, but she recognized the Senator's daughter, Margaret, who sat beside him and seemed impressed by the celebrated people around them.

An eye caught hers—and a smile—and Mrs. Roosevelt

nodded at Amelia Gibson, the wife of the junior Senator from Idaho, Senator Vance Gibson.

Senator Gibson, though still in his first term, was widely regarded as one of the young Westerners whose growing influence was welcome by some and damned by others. The First Lady's eye turned to the Senator. Why he should impress people as a coming young man was immediately apparent. He was handsome and personable, but more than that he was one of those rare men who . . . who once met was never forgotten. Like Franklin D. Roosevelt.

He had made his name, she recalled, as a trial lawyer. He was not as young as he looked; he had practiced law long enough to make a region-wide reputation and a not-inconsiderable fortune. Besides, he had married well. Amelia McCabe Gibson was daughter and heiress of Hale "Scotty" McCabe, who had accumulated ten fortunes as a silver miner and cattleman. Though the Senator could readily have afforded a handsome home in, say, Georgetown, it was Mrs. Gibson's money that had purchased the estate in Fairfax County, Virginia, where she and the Senator presided over a fox hunt which, among other elements of their lives, was, as detractors said, totally inconsistent with anything either of them had known in Idaho.

Amelia McCabe Gibson had impressed Mrs. Roosevelt most favorably. She was short, not more than five-feet-four, and she was fat. Fat was the only word for her. She was not just chubby or plump: she was fat. She had a big soft bosom, a big soft belly, and big soft hips and legs. What so impressed the First Lady was the way Amelia Gibson carried her unstylish self: with grace and style and good humor. She spent money with designers who obeyed her instructions to make no effort to hide her corpulence. To the contrary, they presented her as she wanted to be presented: as a jolly rotund little woman who was not embarrassed by herself.

Mrs. Roosevelt made a mental note to invite the Gibsons

soon to a more private dinner at the White House. The Senator was also a man with a promising future.

"Governor," said the President to Alfred Landon, "I am thinking of trying to put together a coalition cabinet to make this administration more bipartisan as we present a united front against Hitlerism. I am thinking of appointing some prominent Republicans to key positions."

Lily Pons was happily engaged in conversation with the man to her right, and the President concentrated his attention on Landon.

Alf Landon was a solid little man, maybe the archetypal Midwesterner. His face was square, his hair gray, and he wore round, steel-rimmed eyeglasses. His barber ran clippers high on the sides of his head, maybe to clip away more of the hair that had turned gray. Strands of his longer hair tended to get loose and fall over his forehead. He had run an inept campaign in 1936, FDR thought, but the President was not scornful of him and imagined he had done the best a man could do in the circumstances.

"That can only mean one thing, as I see it, Mr. President," said Landon. "It means you are going to run for a third term."

"Not necessarily," said the President. "Not necessarily at all. *This* term has six months to go—and you know, Governor, those six months could be crucial in the history of the twentieth century. I want to face those six months with the strongest possible combination of dedicated men that I can assemble. I want to leave the next fellow in a position to deal from strength."

"Well, it's an admirable idea, Mr. President."

"I thought you could give me some suggestions. I speak in confidence. I am thinking of a Republican Secretary of War and Secretary of the Navy."

Landon's head snapped around, and he stared the President squarely in the face. " 'Key positions' . . ." he said quietly.

"That's what I'm thinking about."

Landon's attention was diverted for a moment. Gibson, the Senator from Idaho, had just risen at his table and looked unsteady on his feet. Claude Pepper, the Senator from Florida, rose beside him to clasp his arm. Senator Gibson smiled warmly and shrugged him off. He walked out of the dining room, obviously unsteady. Mrs. Gibson watched him go and spoke animatedly to the others around their table.

The President too had noticed. "Another guest felled by that damned cheap wine that comes up from the White House pantry," he muttered.

"Looks a little ill," said Landon.

"Well— I thought you might be able to suggest prominent Republicans who might consider—"

"Mr. President," Landon interrupted. "The thing would be much easier if this were not an election year. Any Republican who accepted a position in your cabinet would have to wonder if he were not strengthening the Democratic ticket for 1940."

"I have to consider whether or not I am conceding that no Democrat is qualified to administer national defense policy."

"Do you have any specific Republicans in mind, Mr. President?"

"I do indeed, Governor."

"May I ask who?"

The President grinned. "Why, you of course, Governor," he said. "I think you'd make a capital Secretary of War."

"With every possible respect for you, Mr. President, I must disagree. I don't think I'd make a good Secretary of War at all. I've had no experience—"

"In all frankness, I was thinking as much of national unity as your particular fitness for the office," said the President.

"We could bring in experienced men to serve as your subordinates—and understand, please, I don't mean to make you the titular head of a department run by Democrats. You would choose your subordinates."

"I must respectfully decline, Mr. President," said Landon flatly. "Speaking candidly, I must continue to hope that a Republican will succeed you here next January."

"I appreciate your candor."

"I will, with the same candor, say something else—in confidence. Though I hope a Republican wins in November, I also hope you will run for the third term. If your successor can't be a Republican, then your successor must be you. I believe that a Republican like Bob Taft, for one, has the courage and integrity to face the crisis. Besides yourself, I don't see any Democrat who does."

"And you will speak against me throughout the campaign, using the argument that a third term is a dangerous precedent."

Landon nodded grimly.

"Your gritty honesty would make you a fine Secretary of War, Governor," said the President. He chuckled and patted Landon's shoulder. "It might even have made you a halfway decent President."

The First Lady kept an eye on Amelia Gibson. The young woman continued to talk at the dinner table, apparently gaily, but she glanced toward the door every few seconds.

"What do you suppose was wrong with Gibson?" asked Stimson.

Mrs. Roosevelt shook her head. "Something he ate, I suppose. I hope not here."

"Hmmh . . ." murmured Stimson.

"I think I should send an usher to inquire."

"His wife is leaving the table. I judge she is going to inquire."

"Turning our conversation away from crisis," said Mrs. Roosevelt, "I should like to ask if you have read Mr. Hemingway's new novel *For Whom the Bell Tolls?*"

"I have not, but I know the origin of the title."

"Indeed . . . It is a literary allusion—"

"John Donne," said Stimson, and he recited—

"No man is an Island, entire of itself; every man is a piece of the continent, a part of the main. If a clod be washed away by the sea, Europe is the less, as well as if a promontory were, as well as if a manor of thy friend's or of thine own were. Any man's death diminishes me because I am involved in mankind, and therefore never send to know for whom the bell tolls; it tolls for thee."

"Mr. Stimson! Of course, I remember now, too."

"Part of an elementary education," said Stimson dryly. "I could only wish—"

They were interrupted by a shrill and repeated scream, coming from outside the State Dining Room, from somewhere not far away in the White House.

The President had at hand a microphone, the one he had spoken into when he offered the opening toast; and now he said, "Please, please! Whatever it is, we can't remedy it by rushing out of here. Please stay where you are. We have staff to look into it."

Nevertheless, Mrs. Roosevelt slipped away from the table and crossed the south end of the dining room to the door to the Red Room. She walked through the Red Room and out into the Cross Hall, the main central hall of the White House.

The screaming continued. It came from the East Room.

Three ushers stood in the door to the East Room, conspicuously horrified. As the First Lady walked toward the

East Room, Gerald Baines of the Secret Service bolted into the hall, having run up the stairs from the Ground Floor.

Mrs. Roosevelt reached the door to the East Room. The ushers, astonished to see the First Lady, stepped back.

She stopped in the door.

Lying on his back on the floor, his clothes drenched in blood, lay Senator Vance Gibson. Amelia Gibson knelt beside him, her own skirt soaking up his blood which was on the floor. She screamed again, then again.

II

Mrs. Roosevelt rushed to the frenzied young woman, Amelia Gibson. Not just her dress but her white kid gloves were red with her husband's blood. The First Lady knelt beside her and put her arms around her, staining her own clothes with blood.

The Senator was dead. There could be no doubt about that. Nor could there be any doubt about how he had died. His throat was cut all the way across—"from ear to ear" the cliché was—and his life-blood had gushed out. He lay on his back, eyes wide open as if they stared at the ceiling of the East Room.

"Mr. Baines," said Mrs. Roosevelt. She had worked with Baines before and knew him for a careful, conservative agent of the Secret Service. "May I assume you are in command of the situation?"

Baines, a solid fifty-year-old man with a bullet head and a grave demeanor, nodded. "Yes, ma'am, to the extent that anyone is in command. I would like your consent to telephone Captain Kennelly."

Captain Edward Kennelly was chief of the homicide division, District of Columbia Police. He had worked in the

White House several times. The function of the Secret Service was to protect the President and his family, not to act as detectives to solve crimes, and on a number of occasions Ed Kennelly, once Lieutenant Kennelly, now Captain Kennelly, had brought, not just his police powers, but his skills and understanding, to the solution of crimes that occurred in the White House.

"By all means, Mr. Baines," said Mrs. Roosevelt.

She urged Amelia Gibson to rise. She whispered to her— "Come, dear. We can do nothing here. Let me take you to where we will have privacy and you can—"

Amelia looked up into her eyes and murmured, "Where I can collapse."

"Yes. Upstairs, in our private rooms."

As Mrs. Roosevelt led the staggering woman out of the East Room and toward the staircase to the Second Floor of the White House, Harry Hopkins hurried toward them. "What do I tell the President?" he asked.

Mrs. Roosevelt glanced at the face of Amelia Gibson, she spoke quietly to Hopkins. "Tell him Senator Gibson is dead. Tell him the Senator has been murdered. Tell him to announce . . . whatever he can. The musicale in the East Room is necessarily canceled. Tell him to face the situation as he knows how."

In their years in the White House, they'd encountered other murders in its celebrated rooms. The White House was not just the home of the President and his family—that, in fact, was almost its least function. It was not just a center of government, either. It was a public building, with little private space, and everything that happened in a community could happen there. Everything . . . Yes, and more, because so few of the people who came and went were ordinary citizens, because so many of them were the movers and shakers of a turbulent nation. In a sense, the White House was more public and potentially more dangerous than a street.

Senator Gibson had not died this evening because he was a citizen of the United States, in which statistically a certain number of people per hundred thousand would be murdered each year. He had died because he was a member of a special class who were at greater hazard because of who they were.

The First Lady formed a quick determination that she would find out who killed the Senator, and why—for the sake of his grieving little widow, if for no other reason.

She led Amelia up the stairs to the Second Floor, then through the Center Hall and to the privacy of the West Sitting Hall. She led her into her own bathroom.

"I suggest you take off your dress, my dear," she said. "I will bring you one of my dressing gowns."

Mrs. Roosevelt took off her own dress; and, deciding that the bloodstains could never be washed out, dropped it on the closet floor, to be discarded. She chose a white dressing gown for herself and a beige one for Amelia.

"Here you are. It will be much too long for you, but . . ."

Amelia had dropped her bloody dress and her kid gloves in the bathtub. She stood at the basin, washing her hands and arms, sobbing gently. She turned, dried her hands quickly, and accepted the gown. She put it on, and it was as bad a fit as Mrs. Roosevelt had suggested: almost a foot too long. Fortunately, it was meant to be worn loose; otherwise she could not have closed it.

"Would you like to stay overnight?" the First Lady asked as she gave Amelia her arm and led her into her study. "We have comfortable guest rooms."

Amelia sat down in the study. She shook her head. "No, thank you. I would rather go home. I . . . I want to be at home."

"I will have a Secret Service agent drive you."

"Our car, and the chauffeur, are waiting outside."

"Ah. Well . . . Would you like to rest awhile before you leave? Would you like a cup of tea or coffee?"

"Actually," said Amelia, "what I would like is a double shot of bourbon."

The First Lady put on a gray knit suit before she led Amelia Gibson, still clad in the beige dressing gown and holding up the skirt with both hands, to the private elevator the President used to move between the private quarters and the Oval Office. She led the trembling young woman through the colonnade and into the West Wing, from which they emerged through the north door. The Secret Service had alerted the Gibson chauffeur, and he was waiting on the driveway with a long dark-blue Packard. Mrs. Roosevelt kissed Amelia gently on the cheek just before she got in the car and told her she would phone her in the morning.

She watched the car pass through the gate onto Pennsylvania Avenue, then turned and walked purposefully back toward the White House. She went to the First Floor.

The White House police had roped off the east end of the Cross Hall, and the rope was guarded by two uniformed officers. A few of the dinner guests still milled about in the hall.

"Eleanor! What in the world is going on?"

The question was asked by Alice Roosevelt Longworth, daughter of Theodore Roosevelt, now a Washington *grande dame*. She stood in the Entrance Hall, probably waiting for her car, imperious as ever, and in her red gown possibly the best-dressed woman at the dinner.

Mrs. Roosevelt stopped to speak with her. "Senator Gibson was murdered in the East Room."

"Well, that's what everyone is saying. But— But how in the world . . . ? And where is Amelia?"

"On her way home to Virginia," said the First Lady. "I

took her upstairs and . . . took care of her. She found the body."

"They say his throat was cut."

"Yes."

"Are there any suspects?"

"Not that I know of. I'm going in to talk with the investigating officers."

"Well," said Alice Longworth, "we can be certain of one thing. That little fat woman didn't kill him. She couldn't have had the strength. Or the quickness of movement it would have taken to . . . Well. You see what I mean."

"I see what you mean. Will you excuse me?"

The policemen let down the velvet rope to let the First Lady pass. As the remaining guests gawked, she opened the doors to the East Room just enough to let herself in and closed them quickly. Even so, those who stared got a glimpse of the body lying on the floor.

Gerald Baines rose from one of the chairs that had been arranged for the guests to hear Lily Pons. Captain Edward Kennelly interrupted a conversation he was having with the medical examiner and came toward Mrs. Roosevelt.

"Ah, Mrs. Roosevelt!" he said, extending his hand. "I could only wish we saw each other on happier occasions."

"I, too, Captain Kennelly. I am glad you are here, though."

Kennelly was a big, ruddy-faced Irish cop. He spoke with a brogue. "I am afraid this is a messy one," he said. "There'll be no way of keepin' it confidential. I'm afraid we'll have to confront the boys from the newspapers, sooner or later."

"Yes," she sighed. "I'm afraid that is true. It is a quite *sensational* crime, too, unfortunately."

Kennelly nodded. "Well, we start off knowin' one thing for sure," he said. "We know the cause of death. And we have the weapon."

The First Lady glanced at the body, which remained uncovered. "The cause of death is quite obvious, isn't it? And the weapon?"

Kennelly reached into his jacket pocket and pulled out an object wrapped in a handkerchief. It was a straight razor. "It's been checked for fingerprints," he said. "None on it. None at all. But it wasn't very cleverly hidden. Look—"

He pointed at the floor. A trail of blood stained the parquet. Not drops of blood. Several smears, as if someone had stepped in the blood and smeared it with their feet. They led down the aisle that had been formed when the chairs were placed for the performance by Lily Pons. They led toward the piano, which was situated for her accompanist.

"The razor was in the piano," said Kennelly.

"Is there blood on it?" asked Mrs. Roosevelt.

"It had been wiped once, I think, across his shirt," said Kennelly. "But a little blood remains on it."

"So," said the First Lady. "We know how the Senator was killed and with what weapon. All that remains is the simple question, who did it? Has your investigation produced any evidence on that question?"

"None whatever," said Kennelly.

"Mr. Baines . . . ?"

"I think Ben Washington's statement is useful."

"Ben . . . ? Oh. The usher?"

Baines nodded. He pointed toward a conspicuously apprehensive black man sitting stiffly erect on a chair against the south wall. He beckoned, and Ben Washington rose and came toward them, keeping his eyes averted from the bloody corpse.

"Ben," said Baines. "Tell Mrs. Roosevelt what you told me."

Ben Washington was a tall, spare man, noticed by the First Lady for several years as a man of singular dignity. If in fact any man could be called the ideal White House usher, it might have been this man. He stood erect before her now, clad in his usher's uniform, complete with white cotton gloves.

"The Senator," he said gravely, "come out of the dining room lookin' sick, I mean, he sort of stumbled. I hurry over to him and ask if I can help him. No, he said, he jus' need to go to the bathroom. I point to the stairs and tell him the nearest men's room is right down at the bottom of them stairs. He say he knows. I ask him again if I can help. No, he say. He jus' needs go to the bathroom. I never seed him again. That is, alive I never seed him again. I had my work to do and went on about it. I never seed him till I heard Miz Gibson scream."

"Was there anyone else in the hall or in the East Room, that you saw?" asked Mrs. Roosevelt.

"No, Ma'am. I din't see nobody in dis end. The servin' people come up and down from the kitchen to the dining room through the butler's pantry, and there was lots of traffic there. But those folks don't come out in the hall. An' me, I went back in the usher's room, which don't got a view into this end of the hall, you know."

"During a state dinner the Cross Hall can be deserted," said Baines. "One of the uniformed policemen is always on duty in the vestibule, in case anyone arrives from the North Portico. An usher is on duty to meet anyone who comes in and escorts him to the room where he's supposed to be. But in the Cross Hall itself . . ." He shook his head.

"In other words, the murderer could have arrived at the East Room by any one of half a dozen possible routes and escaped the same way," said Mrs. Roosevelt.

"It had to be someone who had access to the White House," said Baines. "You can't just walk in."

"In other words, the Senator was killed by someone who—"

"Could get in," Kennelly interrupted.

"A thousand people," said Baines unhappily.

"No," said Mrs. Roosevelt, shaking her head emphatically. "Getting in meant nothing unless . . . unless the murderer somehow knew that Senator Gibson would leave the State Dining Room in the middle of a dinner and for some reason come to the East Room. That is too much of a coincidence. I think we have to suppose the Senator left his table at a specific time, perhaps pretending to be ill, and came to the East Room to meet someone. He met his killer by arrangement, not by chance."

"He met someone who had access to the White House," said Baines.

"Or managed to enter without authorization," said the First Lady. "That has happened before."

"The whole thing turns on one point," said Kennelly.

"And what point is that, Captain?"

"Motive," said Kennelly. "Who wanted Senator Gibson dead? And why?"

"Which expands the investigation tremendously," said Mrs. Roosevelt sadly. "We will have to look into the man's life."

It was true that this investigation could not be kept from the attention of the newspapers. So heavy was the pressure from editors and reporters that the President decided to hold a press conference in mid-morning of the next day, Thursday.

The reporters crowded into the Oval Office, a few senior and privileged ones seated, most standing in a semicircle around the President's desk. He opened with a statement—

"As you all know, Vance Gibson was a fine young senator, a man we had learned to respect, whose future seemed unlimited. His death is a tragedy for our country as well as for his state—and of course especially for his family. Mrs. Roosevelt will be calling on his widow this afternoon to convey my personal sympathy, along with her own. It is particularly distressing that his death should have occurred here in the White House. The investigation is being handled by three agencies: the White House police force, the Secret Service, and the homicide squad of the District of Columbia Police Department. I am told by all of them that as of this moment they have no real clue as to who committed the horrible crime. I am afraid that is all I have to tell you."

"Mr. President, could Senator Gibson's bill to impose regulations on the insurance industry have anything to do with his death?"

"I have no reason to think so, and I think it would be improper for us to speculate on anything like that," said the President.

"Mr. President, in the past the First Lady has taken an active role in the investigation of some crimes that took place in the White House or on the grounds. Will she be active in this investigation?"

The President leaned back in his chair and laughed. "My wife's predilection for playing Sherlock Holmes has been immensely exaggerated. If she has any information about this matter—and I am certain she does not—she will inform the official investigators. That's all she's ever done, in fact—that plus suggest a few promising lines of analysis to the official investigators. On the other hand, I did notice she put a big magnifying glass in her handbag this morning."

Having telephoned to be sure she would not be intruding, Mrs. Roosevelt set out for the Gibson estate in Virginia shortly after lunch. Gerald Baines and Ed Kennelly were with her in the blue Buick she drove herself.

The estate was called Fairlea—"lea" being the English word for meadow (as in Gray's "Elegy Written in a Country Churchyard," "The lowing herd wind slowly o'er the lea"). Behind the house, a vast meadow sloped down to Bull Run. In front it was approached by a lane that ran through another meadow. The house itself had been built late in the eighteenth century and repeatedly remodeled by subsequent owners. It was meant to be reminiscent of a Sussex manor house, and fortunately the many remodelers had enlarged it and modernized it but retained its distinctive style. A stone house with a blue slate roof, it was marked by a dozen graceful chimneys, no two exactly alike.

Mrs. Roosevelt had seen Fairlea once before, as the guest of Senator and Amelia Gibson. A horseman herself, she had been surprised at how gracefully and with what authority over her horse the plump Amelia rode. They rode to hounds and had invited the First Lady to join them on a hunt. Mrs. Roosevelt had declined, saying she did not ride well enough for fox hunting.

Amelia had been riding that morning. ("I had to. I had to do *something.*") She wore jodhpurs, boots, and a gray sweater as she greeted Mrs. Roosevelt, Baines, and Kennelly at the door.

She led them straight through the house, to the terrace at the rear. There she invited them to sit down on wrought-iron furniture, and she ordered the butler to bring the cocktail cart.

The butler bent over her and whispered something in her ear. Amelia shot a peremptory finger toward the second floor, south wing.

The view from the terrace was magnificent. The haze-softened outline of the Blue Ridge was visible in the far distance.

"Well . . ." said Amelia softly. "A different life begins today." She closed her eyes for a moment, and her breath shuddered. She threw out her hands. "What good is all this . . . now?"

"I am afraid there is nothing we can say that will answer that question or give you any comfort," said Mrs. Roosevelt.

"I wanted fifteen hundred acres, so I would have privacy," said Amelia. She shook her head. "Now what I'm going to have is loneliness."

"It is too early to make decisions," said Mrs. Roosevelt, "but perhaps you should think of moving away."

"We'd only been here four years," said Amelia. "We bought this place and made it what we wanted it to be. He and I agreed that we would never go back to Idaho, even if he wasn't reelected in 1942. This was to be our home, for the rest of our lives. Well . . . It was for *his.*"

The First Lady stared out across the lea behind the house. She thought she spotted a deer in the distance. "I came to offer my condolences," she said. "Also the President's. He asked me to extend to you his deepest personal sympathy."

"Thank him for me."

"Unfortunately," Mrs. Roosevelt continued, "because of the way Senator Gibson died, we have to ask many questions."

"I understand. I expected that."

Mrs. Roosevelt paused as the butler arrived, pushing a cart laden with bottles, glasses, and a bucket of ice. Amelia dismissed him and poured drinks herself. Kennelly gladly accepted Scotch. So did Baines. Mrs. Roosevelt said she would sip at a small glass of sherry, since she did not usually drink anything before evening. Amelia poured herself a double measure of bourbon.

"The first question has to be: do you have any idea what might have motivated someone to murder your husband?"

Amelia nodded. "Please don't understand me to be accusing anyone," she said, "but I can't help but think someone in the insurance industry wanted him dead. You know about the Gibson Bill."

"Yes," said Mrs. Roosevelt.

"My husband secured its enactment in Idaho. It was the foundation of his political career. The insurance companies estimated that it cost them ten million dollars a year, in Idaho alone. Then he appeared before the legislatures in Montana and Oregon, and they adopted something very much like it. When he introduced it in the United States Senate—"

"It threatened the entire insurance industry," said the First Lady.

"Maybe ye'll be so good as to explain to me what ye're talkin' about," said Kennelly, exaggerating his Irish brogue.

"My husband's ambition," said Amelia, "was to have his bill enacted into law as the Policyholder's Protection Act of 1940. It contains many provisions. Let me explain just one. You buy health insurance. You pay your premiums for years and never file a claim. Then you become ill and have to look to the insurer to pay a part of your medical bills. The insurer pays. It has to, under the policy. But the next year, when you try to renew, the company either drops you utterly and refuses to insure you, or it doubles or triples your premium. In other words, they collect your premiums happily as long as you never get sick and use your insurance to pay your bills; but if you do, they don't want you anymore. My husband's bill forbade that. Under the Gibson Bill, if you have been insured by a health-insurance company for one year, the company cannot refuse to insure you for subsequent years. It can increase your premiums reasonably as you get older and are a greater risk, but only as it increases them for everyone your age."

"That is only one of the provisions of the bill," said Mrs. Roosevelt. "The insurance industry shrieks in horror."

"Once," said Amelia, "my husband introduced in the Idaho legislature a bill he regarded as entirely facetious and did not expect to be given serious attention. It would have outlawed the name 'insurance company.' Companies that sold insurance would have had to go under the name 'So-and-so Premium Collecting and Policyholder Gouging Company.' The companies had no sense of humor about it."

"And he built a political career on it," said Kennelly. "Good for him!"

"They may have killed him," said Amelia solemnly.

"I assume," said Baines, "they have unlimited resources."

"Yes, and they spent hundreds of thousands of dollars trying to defeat him when he ran for the Senate," said Amelia. "They've spent money since, trying to discredit him."

"In addition," said Mrs. Roosevelt, "he voted against the Neutrality Act and in general stood up for every proposal by the President to throw our country's weight into the balance to save Western Civilization. As a result, he was honored by being hated by such organizations as America First and the German-American Bund."

"A sorry loss to our country," said Kennelly.

"Had anyone threatened him, dear?" the First Lady asked.

"Not that he told me."

"Why did he leave the dinner and go out in the hall last night?"

"He said he didn't feel well. He said he was nauseous. I suggested he go to the bathroom. He resisted for a little while—until others around the table joined me in urging him to go out. I offered to go with him, to be sure he made it to the bathroom all right, but he said it was nothing, really, and he'd be okay. He got up and left the table—and I never saw him alive again."

Amelia covered her face with her hands and wept.

Mrs. Roosevelt put her hand on Amelia's shoulder. "I am sorry, dear. We shouldn't have come so soon with our questions."

"I *want* to answer all the questions you can ask," Amelia whispered tearfully through her hands. "I want you to find out who killed Vance."

"We—"

Amelia interrupted. "After he'd been gone three or four minutes, I decided to go and see about him, even though he'd told me I didn't need to. I've been a guest in the White

House a few times, so I knew where he would have gone: to the east stairs and down to the men's room on the Ground Floor. I hurried through the Cross Hall and . . . I hadn't passed the door to the Blue Room when I saw him! He was lying on the floor just inside the East Room. I thought he'd collapsed. I ran the rest of the way. And when I came through those doors, I saw— You know what I saw."

"I'm sorry," said Mrs. Roosevelt, "but I must think about time. How much time do you think passed between Senator Gibson's leaving your table and your finding him?"

Amelia shook her head. "What did I say? Three minutes? Four?"

"Not time enough for him to have gone to the men's room downstairs and come back up," said Mrs. Roosevelt.

"I suppose not."

"Have you any idea why he went into the East Room?"

"No idea."

"We have to consider," said Mrs. Roosevelt, "the possibility that he was not ill but only feigned illness, so he could go to the East Room to keep a prearranged appointment."

"With whom?"

"If we knew, we would know who killed him," said the First Lady.

"But he *was* nauseous. Could he have faked such a thing?"

"Think of it. Could he?"

"Well, it was odd that he became suddenly ill. He had been in rosy good health. He'd been chatting comfortably with the others at the table. He— Oh, God!"

"You see," said Mrs. Roosevelt, "we have to doubt such a strange coincidence. Senator Gibson suddenly becomes ill at table. He leaves the dining room and goes to the East Room, where he confronts someone who killed him. How could his murderer have guessed he would come there at that time?"

"I'm ready to think," said Kennelly, "it was not a murderer but *murderers*. The Senator was a strong man, I guess. Someone must have grabbed him and held him while the other one— Well . . . while the other one did what the other one did."

"Pursuing the question of whether or not he was ill," said Mrs. Roosevelt, "I should like to know if you saw any sign of illness in him the night before. I mean, did he—"

Amelia shook her head. "We weren't together Tuesday night," she said. "It's a long drive between here and the Capitol. We keep an apartment in Georgetown. Vance was there Tuesday night. I met him at the White House."

"Did you spend many nights apart?" asked Kennelly.

"As a matter of fact, yes. Three nights a week, typically. His duties on the Hill kept him in his office until rather late many evenings. I can't tell you I preferred our little apartment to this house. We furnished it handsomely, but it is very small: just a foyer, living room, kitchen, bedroom, and bath. So when he stayed at the apartment, sometimes I came into Washington to be with him, and sometimes I didn't. Particularly when the weather is warm and I can ride and swim here."

"Was it lonely out here?" asked Kennelly.

"No. We have many friends. It's a rare night when we don't have a house guest or two. Vance loved to entertain. So do I. Without much modesty, let me say I always enjoyed showing off the estate." She sobbed. *"Used* to."

"I think," said Mrs. Roosevelt, "that we have imposed enough of a burden on you. I think we should go back to Washington."

"You are welcome here," said Amelia. "In fact, I hope you will come and stay a day or two, whenever you can. We share a memory I want to dispel, but—"

"I will return as soon as I can. If I can offer any solace—"

"Oh . . . Oh. One question. When will my husband's body be released?"

"We can do that immediately, Mrs. Gibson," said Kennelly. "Ordinarily we require an autopsy when a man dies violently. But the cause of death is so obvious, I see no reason to do it in this case. I'll arrange to have the remains released this afternoon."

"May I have a funeral director call you?"

"Of course. Here's my card. And let me join Mrs. Roosevelt in offering sympathy. I hope you won't have to talk to another policeman, Mrs. Gibson. And understand we'll do our very best to find out who did this terrible thing."

"I am grateful to you all," said Amelia Gibson.

III

The President enjoyed his cocktail hour that evening with Missy, Ross McIntyre, his physician, and Justice Felix Frankfurter, who had telephoned earlier in the day and said he'd like to have a few minutes conversation with the President.

Mrs. Roosevelt, who was a particular friend of Justice Frankfurter, stopped by just long enough to greet him and sip half a glass of sherry before she hurried on to her rooms to change into the gown she would wear for the evening.

"Any word about the murder?" the President asked.

"Why, of course not," said the First Lady. "I'm not investigating it."

Evidence of the murder still lay on the floor of her closet, where she had left her bloodstained gown from last night. She had put down newspaper on the floor and moved Amelia Gibson's gown and gloves there, too. Her impulsive humanitarian gesture of throwing her arms around the distraught little woman had cost her an expensive dress, a favorite, that she had expected to wear this evening. The two gowns were a distressing sight. She didn't think she should ask a maid to handle them. Walking into her study she picked up an empty carton in which some books had been delivered Monday. She put the two gowns and the gloves in the carton, folded the flaps over the top, and pushed it to the rear of the closet. She would tell a maid to take the box down and have it burned.

In the West Sitting Hall, Justice Frankfurter had turned the conversation to the topic he wanted to discuss. "There is no point in beating about the bush," he said to the President. "I'll simply ask you outright if you've spoken with Harry Stimson."

The President smiled. "You are always his advocate."

"He is one of the most able men in the United States," said Frankfurter. "I know your problems with Secretary of War Woodring. Europe is collapsing, and Washington is a-tittering and a-fluttering. Stimson would bring stability to the War Department."

"Would he accept the appointment?" the President asked.

"He would if he could appoint his own assistant secretary."

"Well, he's going up to Yale to deliver the commencement address in a couple of weeks," said the President. "Let's see what he says. If he says what I suspect he's going to say, he'll be one of our most effective spokesmen for preparedness."

"Which would make him a perfect Secretary of War," said Frankfurter, raising his glass as if to toast.

When Mrs. Roosevelt came out of her rooms, dressed for the affair she was attending that evening, Frankfurter and McIntyre had left and the President sat quietly and thoughtfully with Missy, sipping the last drops of his second martini.

"What gala tonight, Babs?" he asked, tilting his head and admiring her white satin evening dress.

"A benefit for English children being evacuated from London in anticipation of bombing," she said. "They are run-

ning the movie *Gone with the Wind,* and Mr. Clark Gable
and Miss Vivien Leigh will be there, among others."

"My lord, Babs. You'll be there until after midnight."

"No," she said. "They are running the picture now—
have been since five o'clock. Many of the guests for the
reception afterward are not in the theater audience.
Some, like I myself, will arrive only for the cocktails and
hors d'oeuvres."

"Give my regards to whoever's there," he said.

"I hope you retire early, Franklin," said Mrs. Roosevelt.
"You sound tired."

He was more tired by the time he sat propped up on pillows
in his bed half an hour later. Arthur Prettyman had helped
him undress, then to move from his wheelchair into his
bath, later to lift himself from the tub back to the wheelchair, to dress in pajamas, then to climb into bed.

Missy came in. She had been to her own suite on the third
floor, had taken her own bath, and returned in a light blue
nightgown and sheer white peignoir. He picked up the telephone and told the kitchen to send up their dinner trays.
Missy switched on the radio. By coincidence, Lily Pons was
singing in concert in New York, so the President listened to
something of what he had missed last night.

"This murder business is very touchy," remarked Missy.

"I'm sure it is," said the President.

"This one is unusually touchy," she said. "He had quite a
reputation, you know. Senator Gibson . . ."

"For what, womanizing?"

Missy nodded. "He stayed in Georgetown many nights,
when Mrs. Gibson was out in Virginia. There have been
rumors for some time that he didn't spend those nights
alone."

"The newspaper boys won't touch that one, thank God,"
said the President.

"Well . . . They will if it turns out he was killed by a jealous husband."

They ate in silence, listening to the radio concert. When their trays had been taken, Missy asked the President— "Effdee, do you still want to run the movie, or would you rather go to sleep?"

"I've been looking forward to the movie," he said.

The motion picture studios sent sixteen-millimeter versions of many of their movies to the White House for the President to see. He had a Bell & Howell projector on a wheeled stand, and a screen came down from the ceiling. Missy had learned to run the projector. The films were generally not the most recent releases. He had not been offered *Gone with the Wind,* for instance; but that was fine with the President, who enjoyed some of the older films better, anyway.

The film for tonight was *Stagecoach,* the John Ford western that had been released only about a year ago. Missy loaded a big reel on the projector, threaded the film, switched off the lights, and started the picture.

The President plumped his pillows and settled back comfortably to watch. Missy tossed the peignoir aside and climbed onto the bed beside him, propping herself up on her own pillows. The President caressed her leg affectionately, and she put her face to his neck and kissed him under the ear. The screen credits were finished now, and they relaxed and focused their attention on the screen.

Gerald Baines was never comfortable entering someone else's home as an intruder, official intruder though he might be. It didn't seem to bother Ed Kennelly, who had used a skeleton key to unlock the door to the Gibson apartment in Georgetown.

"He lived well here, too," said Baines as he looked around the apartment.

The door opened onto a foyer, furnished with an umbrella stand, a coat tree, a marble-topped table, and a large mirror. A Chinese vase sat on the table. A painting Baines recognized as a Van Gogh—of iris blooms in a vase—hung on one wall.

Kennelly switched on lights, entirely careless of how conspicuous this would be to neighbors who would see lights coming on in the apartment of a man they knew had been murdered.

The living room was elegantly furnished in French Art Deco design. The room was paneled in palisander and olive wood, except for one wall that was covered by a marquetry panel in an abstract geometric design in red, orange, and olive green and another wall dominated by a frosted-glass window framed with aluminum. Corner bookcases stood in each corner of the room, also of the same woods. An olive-wood desk sat by the window. Beneath the marquetry panel sat a simple couch with cylindrical cushions at each end. To the right of the couch was a big overstuffed easy chair. An octagonal pedestal table served as coffee table to the couch and smoking stand for the chair.

Obviously, the room had been designed somewhere else and installed in this apartment. Likely, it had been Senator Gibson's intention to take the room with him—not just the furniture but the paneling and marquetry—when he gave up the place.

Oddly, elegance ended at the bedroom door. The one bedroom looked as if it had been furnished from Sears, Roebuck, with a steel bed finished to look like grained wood and not really looking like it at all. The night table by the bed was of ugly yellow oak. But the chair—the chair in the bedroom was an Empire piece, possibly a genuine antique, possibly a reproduction: a graceful gilded chair upholstered in peach-colored silk, with two swans of ebonized wood serving as arms.

If Kennelly was impressed, he concealed it. He went

about the rooms, looking at this and that, occasionally writing a note in a little pad. He used a toothpick from his jacket pocket to lift two cigarette butts from an ashtray on the octagonal table and deposit them in a white envelope.

"How long were we with Mrs. Gibson this afternoon?" he asked Baines.

"What? An hour? A little more . . ."

"How many cigarettes did she smoke in that hour?"

Baines shook his head. "I don't remember seeing her smoke any."

"No, neither did I. But the butts I just picked up are of two different brands: Camels and Herbert Tareytons." He shrugged. "Maybe another senator was here, and the two men smoked while they talked. Or maybe—"

"Maybe it was a woman," said Baines. "Is there lipstick on—?"

"No."

Kennelly strode into the bedroom. He frowned over the ashtray on the night table. "Okay. Camels and Tareytons. If two senators smoked these two brands, we've got a *damned* interesting suggestion here. I'd rather think it was a woman."

Baines shook his head. "If it were another woman, why do we find the butts?" he asked. "Wouldn't the Senator have flushed them down, so Mrs. Gibson wouldn't find what we've just found?"

"Good point . . . I wonder how often Mrs. Gibson came here."

"Well," said Baines, "I believe she said this afternoon she didn't like the apartment much, particularly when the weather is good and she can ride and swim at Fairlea."

"On the other hand," said Kennelly, "she must have had a key and could walk in here any time she wanted to, announced or unannounced. Wasn't it careless of him to leave someone else's cigarette butts lying around?"

"Argues against the idea it was a woman," said Baines.

Kennelly went into the kitchen. "Settled," he said.

Dishes remained in the sink: two glasses, two plates, two forks.

"But how could he have been so careless?" Baines persisted. "His wife could have come here any time. In town shopping, wanted to freshen up . . . Wanted to use the bathroom . . ."

Kennelly went in the bathroom. "Curiouser and curiouser," he said. "Nothing that suggests a woman. No comb. No brush. No perfume. No lipstick . . . Just the things a man uses. But—"

He used a bit of toilet tissue to pick up a yellow-red-black tube of Ipana toothpaste which he shoved into another white envelope.

Kennelly opened two closet doors and the drawers in the bedroom bureau. "Now, here's something odd, too," he said. "There's only one set of sheets and pillowcases: the ones on the bed. Didn't the man keep a second set? Hey, and look at something else. No spare towels or washcloths. Just what's hanging on the racks. Is that odd? Why would a man have only one set of—"

"Let's don't speculate," said Baines.

"No. Look at that bed. It could have been slept in by one man alone, but if it was, he was a man who used all the pillows and rolled all over the bed. Proves nothing. He could have been a restless sleeper."

"Okay," said Baines. "We conclude a woman slept here with him Tuesday night. Who?"

"It would be helpful to know," said Kennelly.

Gone with the Wind had but ten minutes to run when the First Lady arrived at the theater. The crowd on the street applauded as she left her car and went inside—though it was apparent that who they wanted to see was Clark Gable and Vivien Leigh, not Mrs. Roosevelt, however well they did or did not think of her.

She was led through the first-floor lobby of the big motion-picture house: all red-carpeted and perhaps baroque or rococo, though probably neither. On the second-floor lobby an elaborate display of hors d'oeuvres was spread over four tables, and a fully stocked bar awaited thirsty guests.

Because the benefit was for English children, English stars predominated in the crowd that waited for the appearance, not just of the First Lady but also of Gable and Leigh. That meant that Laurence Olivier was there, as was Charles Chaplin and Stanley Laurel, Sir Cedric Hardwicke, Boris Karloff and Rex Harrison, and others. There was in Hollywood a community of English players, and many of them had come to Washington tonight. Some had come from London, where the West End had pledged itself to continue to offer shows as long as a single theater remained standing.

"It is inconceivable to me," said Mrs. Roosevelt to Boris Karloff—whose real name was William Henry Pratt—"that bombs should fall on London."

"They fell there in the last war," said Boris Karloff. "From the zeppelins, you will recall."

The actor who had played Frankenstein's monster and other monsters and murderers as well, was in person a craggy-faced, beetle-browed man but soft-spoken and gentle of personality.

"Oh, the zeppelins, I do remember," said Mrs. Roosevelt. "As I recall, most of their bombs fell in Regent's Park."

Karloff nodded. "They mistook the reflection of the moon on Boating Lake as its reflection on the Thames and dropped their bombs into the park, thinking they were dropping them on the London docks."

Not long after, she spoke with Charles Chaplin. "David Niven went back and enlisted, you know," he said. "The British ambassador, Lord Lothian, told him the best service he could do his country was to stay in Hollywood and give

British people a sympathetic character on the screen. But he went back and is serving in a Highland regiment. He's a Scot, you know. I wish I could serve. But I'm fifty-one years old. They say war is a young man's business."

Mrs. Roosevelt nodded. "My son Elliott is already serving. If war comes, the other boys will go. I know they will."

Chaplin reached for a waiter's tray and neatly plucked off a glass of champagne for the First Lady. "I was sorry to read of the death of Senator Gibson. I've twice been a guest at Fairlea. Mrs. Gibson—Amelia—enjoys having movie people as her guests. So did he. Westerners, you know. Fascinated with the silver screen. I understand that Greta Garbo spends weekends at Fairlea."

"It's a lovely estate," said Mrs. Roosevelt.

"They are interesting people," said Chaplin. "Amelia is not everyone's idea of an American beauty, but she is a vital, fascinating woman. They were a matched pair. I can't imagine how she is going to live without him."

"When you say they were a matched pair—"

"Oh, I mean that they were characteristic American Westerners. He grew up on a ranch, a large farm at least. He was an expert horseman, as is she, but when they moved to Virginia she insisted he learn to ride English style. Her father was a flamboyant character. He became extremely wealthy. The family lived in a huge Victorian mansion in Boise, which he bought late in life; and Amelia likes to tell the story that he enjoyed startling his guests by drawing a six-shooter and expertly shooting the tips off the candles on the parlor mantel."

"An exaggeration, I feel certain," said Mrs. Roosevelt.

"Well, she is an interesting combination of western rusticity and Virginia hunt-country sophistication," said Chaplin. "The Senator remained a little rougher and was sometimes heard complaining to Amelia that she 'put on airs.' "

"I feel immensely sympathetic for the poor young woman," said Mrs. Roosevelt.

"As do I," said Chaplin.

Mrs. Roosevelt had several times met Stanley Laurel, the English vaudevillian who had endeared himself to American artists as the small, self-effacing partner in the team of Laurel and Hardy. She felt strongly drawn to the man, who was not much different in person from the character he played on the screen. They were chatting amiably when a disturbance on the street, audible inside the theater, told them Clark Gable and Vivien Leigh had arrived.

King and queen of the movies that year, they made a regal entrance. When they reached the top of the stairs they were led immediately to the First Lady.

Captain Edward Kennelly and Agent Gerald Baines interrupted their work in mid-evening to take dinner at Harvey's, one of Washington's finest restaurants. It was expensive, said Kennelly, but chances were they wouldn't receive a check. The management was known for "losing" the checks of men prominent in law enforcement. He didn't take advantage of this, Kennelly said, but did dine there two or three times a year, never more.

J. Edgar Hoover, Director of the F.B.I., and his associate and boyfriend Clyde Tolson ate there every evening. They were in fact at their usual table when Kennelly and Baines came in.

"Good evening, Captain," Hoover said, standing and extending his hand. "And . . . Mr. Baines, I believe?"

"Good evening, Director," said Kennelly. "Clyde."

"I understand you are working on the case of the murder of Senator Vance Gibson," said Hoover. "Is there anything we can do to help?"

"I'm pleased that you asked, Director," said Kennelly. "I expect to lift some fingerprints later this evening. I'd like to have them run through your files as quickly as possible. Would it be possible to have them run tonight?"

"Absolutely," said Hoover. "Clyde will call headquarters as soon as we finish dinner and tell the duty officer to see to it that your fingerprints are processed tonight. Is it an important lead? Or should I ask?"

"Feel welcome to ask," said Kennelly. "My answer has to be, I don't know. It's a shot in the dark that may prove something but more than likely won't."

"Anything we can do for you, be sure to call," said Hoover.

"We appreciate it. And we will."

When he and Baines were seated at their table, Kennelly said, "Even that little favor may cost us. If we find any useful prints on the tube of Ipana I've got in my pocket, you can bet Hoover will call a press conference and announce that the F.B.I. broke the case."

"You don't like him, do you?"

"We had a real problem with him last year, when we broke the case of the murder of Congressman Garber's son. Hoover and Tolson ran wild. All they want is credit, publicity. They're a pair of . . . you-know-what. They make me sick!"

Even so, when the two men came to F.B.I. headquarters about ten o'clock, carrying the fingerprints the D.C. police lab had lifted from the tube of toothpaste, they found that the Director or Tolson had called, true to their word, and the prints were immediately run through the central files of fingerprints from all over the United States. The process took about half an hour.

The technician was a young man, correctly dressed to Bureau standards, even at this hour, in a dark suit, white shirt, and tightly knotted necktie.

"As you noticed," he said, "there are two sets of fingerprints on the tube. They are rather badly smudged. Squeezing a tube of toothpaste, you tend to run your finger and thumb back and forth. Fortunately, it gives a clear print of the thumb but a badly smudged print of the index or middle finger. Anyway . . . what we have here is clear identification of Senator Vance Gibson. He squeezed the tube. As to the other set of prints, we have no record of them. They were left on the tube by a person whose fingerprints have never been taken and sent here."

Kennelly nodded. "Do you have Mrs. Gibson's prints on file?"

The young technician smiled. "As a matter of fact, we do. Mrs. Amelia Gibson seems to have had a singular contempt for Prohibition. She was arrested once in Idaho, at the Canadian border, in 1928, carrying a dozen cases of Scots whisky in her car. She was arrested on the same charge again in 1930, in Washington. The charges were dropped both times, but her fingerprints were taken." He shook his head. "The prints on that tube of Ipana are not hers."

Kennelly looked to Baines and chuckled. "Figured," he said.

Both Baines and Kennelly were accustomed to the fact that the First Lady kept long hours, especially when her attention was fastened on anything; so neither was surprised to find waiting for them at D.C. police headquarters a message to telephone her if they arrived there before midnight. Kennelly called, and she asked if he were too tired to sit down over a snack in the White House pantry and discuss the Gibson case.

"I am anxious that we should resolve this case as soon as possible," she said when they were together, not in fact in the pantry but in the kitchen on the Ground Floor. "I mean, I am anxious that *you* should resolve it. I am only tangentially involved. But you do understand that the press is aware of this murder and will demand facts sooner rather than later."

She had changed out of her white satin gown and had come down to the kitchen dressed in a nightgown and a long blue woolen robe. They sat around the big central table where food was prepared. The night man in the kitchen had brought out a loaf of bread and a platter of assorted meats, plus mustard and ketchup. He had a pot of coffee steaming. A pot of coffee was kept steaming in the White House kitchen day and night. Mrs. Roosevelt suggested, though, that the two men might like whisky or beer. Baines had accepted a shot of Scotch. Kennelly let the man pour gin over ice.

"New facts?" she asked. "I've been occupied this evening."

"Only one fact," said Kennelly. "Someone besides the Senator shared his Georgetown apartment. We have no idea who. We have strange fingerprints from a tube of toothpaste: not the Senator's, not Mrs. Gibson's. Besides the Senator, someone else used that tube of toothpaste. Tomorrow morning a team from headquarters will go over everything in that apartment, looking for prints. We found two kinds of cigarette butts. But Mrs. Gibson doesn't seem to smoke."

"Have we given any attention to the question of who besides Senator Gibson left the dining room at approximately the same time he did?"

"Yes," said Baines. "And I've spoken on the telephone to Senator Claude Pepper, who was at the same table with the Gibsons. He confirms all that Mrs. Gibson says: that the Senator became ill and asked to be excused, and so forth. He has no idea why the Senator became ill. Anyway— To find out who else left the room, we have to identify at least one person from each table and ask the question. We've used the seating plan, and agents have been calling. The difficulty with that, of course, is that you may be telephoning the very person who—"

"Who doesn't want it known that he or she left the table," said the First Lady.

"Besides, ma'am, most of them are rather prominent people. They are not easy to reach, and some of them are a little hostile about being asked."

"Any names so far?" she asked.

"Well, Congressman Carl Vinson went down to the men's room about five minutes before the Senator went, so far as we can fix the time. It would be helpful if he'd seen the Senator down there, but he didn't. He didn't see anybody else either."

Mrs. Roosevelt shook her head. "Do any of the ushers confirm having seen him go down?"

"No, ma'am. It's difficult to believe, isn't it, how deserted the halls can be when there's a big state dinner going on? But it's true. I've worked in the White House many years. Our security depends on covering the entrances. We don't patrol. Neither do the uniformed police until after everyone has retired. It seems intrusive. It's traditional that we don't do it."

"Have you identified anyone else who left the State Dining Room during the significant period?"

"Yes, ma'am. So far one more. Mrs. Everett Dirksen, wife of a Republican congressman from Illinois. She went to the powder room during the significant period. But . . . Well, she saw no one either, not downstairs or upstairs—except of course the usher."

"Allow me," said Mrs. Roosevelt, "to offer a suggestion. If we assume that the murderer was downstairs, we ignore a real possibility—which is that the murderer was *upstairs* and came *down* to kill the Senator, after which he escaped by returning upstairs."

"The Second Floor, where your private quarters are, ma'am, is more closely watched than the public rooms on the First Floor. All rooms west of the Stair Hall are always covered. The President's study and your private rooms are always guarded."

"Even so," said Mrs. Roosevelt, "someone could have come up the main stairs and turned east. He could have hidden in the Lincoln Suite or in the Queen's Bedroom until opportunity afforded itself to escape from the house."

"*If* he escaped from the house," said Kennelly.

"Captain Kennelly," said the First Lady, "except for the President and myself, when we don't have family or other guests, only two people *live* in the White House: my husband's private and confidential secretary, Miss LeHand, and Harry Hopkins. Everyone else leaves at night, sooner or later."

"Ah, but . . ." said Kennelly. "Suppose someone who does not live in the White House but who works in it every day . . . Suppose that one person hid out in the White House overnight and appeared at his office the next morning. You see, he didn't have to escape after the murder."

Mrs. Roosevelt shook her head and ran her hands over her eyes. She sighed. Then a faint smile appeared on her face. "People who commit murder don't make it easy to catch them, do they?"

IV

Accompanied by two fingerprint men, Ed Kennelly arrived at the Gibson apartment in Georgetown a little after nine o'clock on Friday morning. He took out his skeleton key to put it in the stupidly simple lock that was supposed to secure an apartment that had valuable items in it—but found the door was ajar.

From inside he heard a female voice singing. The singing voice was so appealing that Kennelly paused at the door and let her finish the song.

> *They asked me how I knew*
> *My true love was true.*
> *I of course replied*
> *Something here inside*
> *Cannot be denied.*
> *They said someday you'll find,*
> *All who love are blind.*
> *When your heart's on fire,*
> *You must realize*
> *Smoke gets in your eyes.*
> *So I chaffed them,*

47

And I gaily laughed,
To think they could know my love . . .
Yet today, my love is gone away.
I am without my love.
Now laughing friends deride
Tears I cannot hide.
So I smile and say,
When a lovely flame dies,
Smoke gets in your eyes.

He walked into the living room. "Kennelly, homicide, District police. Wanta tell me who you are, dear? And how you got in?"

The young black woman who confronted him was strikingly beautiful. She was dressed in the uniform of a housemaid: gray dress and white apron. "I'm Lena Madison," she said. "I work here. I let myself in with the key Senator Gibson gave me."

"You—"

"I clean up the apartment. Every morning." She swung an arm around and indicated empty ashtrays, wastebasket emptied into a brown paper bag, a vacuum cleaner standing in the middle of the room. "Not yesterday. I heard the Senator . . . Well, you know. I figured I shouldn't come yesterday. I figured you'd want to search the place, see it as it was. But today I came and—"

"Have you washed the dishes?" Kennelly asked crisply.

"Yessir."

Ed Kennelly ran his hand over his head, through his hair. "Wiped them dry, I suppose," he said.

"Yessir. Wasn't I supposed to?"

He shook his head. "Well . . . Let's go back to Wednesday. Did you work here Wednesday?"

"Yessir. I came every morning, just about the time the Senator left. Like eight-thirty. Usually some dishes to wash, ashtrays to empty. Get rid of the trash. Not much of it.

Vacuum. Dust. He really didn't need me every day. Lots of times I came, and he hadn't even been here since I left the day before. But he insisted I have to come every day, do the little work the place needed. I guess the Senator was what you would call . . . What's the word? *Fastidious.* Not for me to decide if he really needed the place cleaned six days a week. He paid me to do it. The Senator was strong about Miz Gibson not coming in here and finding the place a mess."

Kennelly sat down in the overstuffed chair. "Sit down, Lena," he said, pointing to the couch.

She sat. Her tight skirt rode up, and he could not help but appreciate her long slender legs. She was the color of coffee-with-cream, with a flawless complexion. Her shiny black hair was long, and she wore it tied behind her head and pinned up. He wondered how it looked when she let it down.

"You guys work the bathroom," he said to the fingerprint men. "Bedroom. Wherever." Turning again to Lena, he asked, "Did you get the impression that Senator Gibson didn't live here alone?"

"Is that my business to think about?" she asked.

"Not until he was murdered," said Kennelly. "Until he was murdered, it wasn't my business to wonder about it, or yours; but now it is our business. Until I find out who killed him, all kinds of things that were private before are suddenly police business. You get me?"

"I get you, uh . . . Lieutenant . . . ?"

"Captain Edward Kennelly."

"Sorry. Captain. Well, it's perfectly obvious why he wanted the place worked on every morning. I never saw a woman. She left early. But there was sometimes plenty of evidence about what had happened the night before."

"Like what?"

"Drinking glasses smelling of liquor. Sometimes just one, from nights he was alone, I suppose. Lots of mornings I'd find two. Two cups and saucers. Two plates with toast crumbs on them. Two kinds of cigarette butts. Then of course the bed. All rumpled. Sheets and pillowcases sometimes smelling of perfume. Two towels used. Two washcloths. My job was to wash the bedclothes and the towels. I carried them home every day in a grocery bag and brought the clean ones back every morning."

Kennelly nodded thoughtfully. He glanced into the kitchen, where the two fingerprint men were working diligently. "Let's see how observant you were, Lena," he said. "What kind of cigarettes did Senator Gibson smoke?"

"Camels."

"Right. And the woman?"

"May have been two women," said Lena. "I've dumped Tareyton butts. And Kools."

"And sometimes the sheets smelled of perfume and sometimes not?"

"Right."

"Do you think he was seeing two women at the same time, or did one follow after the other?"

"The one who smoked Kools and wore perfume used to be the only one. Lately it's been both. The Tareyton one must have got the inside track lately. The Kools one hasn't been here so often the last month or so."

"But you never saw either one of them?"

"No. I guess the Senator was being careful—brought them in late at night and hustled them out of here before dawn."

"Did you ever see Mrs. Gibson?"

"No, sir. In all the time I've worked here, I never saw the lady."

"There's something damned odd here, isn't there, Lena?"

"Yes, sir. There sure is."

"Tell me what you think it is."

The handsome young woman glanced around the apartment and sighed. "Well, sir, when I came in here this morning I expected to find the place just the way I left it Wednesday morning: meaning clean and neat, dishes in the cabinets, not on the kitchen table. He couldn't have slept in his bed Wednesday night. He was killed Wednesday evening. Then the dishes. Two glasses, two plates, two forks. He did something Wednesday he'd never done before. He brought the Tareyton lady here during the day. And they were in bed . . ."

Kennelly nodded. "Exactly. It could be a coincidence that he brought Miss Tareytons here only a few hours before he was murdered. It *could be* a coincidence . . . but that'd be only a little short of fantastic, don't you think?"

"I'm no detective, sir. But suppose he brought her here Wednesday to tell her he was breaking off with her."

"In other words, suppose she killed him because he was breaking off their affair."

Lena nodded. "Suppose that," she said.

"Then why didn't she kill him here?" asked Kennelly.

Lena shrugged. "How? He didn't use a straight razor. Kitchen knife . . . Pretty difficult, that. And if she didn't have a gun in her purse."

He laughed. "You think like Mrs. Roosevelt," he said.

"Guess she'll lose her job, come January—just like I just lost this one here."

The President had traveled by train to Charlottesville, Virginia, where he would deliver the commencement address at the University of Virginia Law School. Franklin, Junior, graduated that day, and the President had long since agreed to give the commencement address.

As France collapsed in the north, Mussolini had decided to claim his share of the spoils by invading from the southeast. Word of the Italian invasion came as the President traveled south on the presidential train, called POTUS—President of the United States. Hastily, he added a few sentences to his speech. State Department advisers on the train recommended he not use the words. But he did—

"Today . . . the hand that held the *dagger* . . . has *struck* it . . . into the *back* . . . of its *neighbor.*"

Privately, to Franklin, Junior, as POTUS rolled through Virginia, he rubbed his hands together and smiled the great, broad Roosevelt smile. "That cheap little Italian *poseur* couldn't have done us a better service," he said. "Tomorrow the isolationist vote in Congress and among the people will diminish by half. I can propose measures for preparedness that I would hardly have dared propose two weeks ago."

Administrative duties occupied more of the First Lady's time than she would have wished. On Friday afternoon she went down to the housekeeper's office to hear a tearful appeal from a waiter who did not want to be fired.

Mrs. Henrietta Nesbitt was the White House housekeeper, a neighbor brought down from Dutchess County in 1933. Though the President scorned Mrs. Nesbitt's unimaginative cuisine, Mrs. Roosevelt admired the way she kept careful control over the housekeeping budget and defended her staunchly against the President's repeated complaints that her state dinners were a disgrace and the daily meals in the house were bland. The First Lady's only complaint of Mrs. Nesbitt was that she was perhaps a bit too stern with the black men and women who worked in the White House.

Sam Carter, out of uniform and seated in Mrs. Nesbitt's office in the shiny black suit of a faithful churchgoer, was tearful. "Ah work in de Whaat House since *1917!*" he sobbed. "Only job Ah evah had. What's—"

"What's going to become of you if you are discharged for drunkenness?"

"Surely, Henrietta—" Mrs. Roosevelt ventured.

"On the night of an important state dinner," said Mrs. Nesbitt. "On Wednesday night, he got staggering drunk and finally passed out. We were fortunate he did it downstairs and not in the State Dining room."

"Ah, no—"

"Do you deny it? You got *drunk* and—"

"How could he get drunk during a White House dinner?" asked the First Lady.

"They all do it," said Mrs. Nesbitt sternly. "As they carry the trays down from the State Dining room, they grab up the half-empty wine glasses and drink the champagne and wine not finished by the guests."

"I am told," said Mrs. Roosevelt slyly, "it was not very good champagne."

Sam Carter shook his head. "It wasn't, ma'am," he said. "Askin' yo' pardon, it wasn't good champagne."

"You sampled the champagne served by the Wilsons, the Hardings, the Coolidges, the Hoovers, and the Roosevelts?"

"Yes, ma'am."

"And ours is the worst?"

Sam Carter shook his head. "Beggin' yo' pardon—"

"What about Prohibition?" asked Mrs. Roosevelt.

He grinned. "Nevah counted in th' Whaat House. Why, Miz Hoover, she had the very finest vintage French—"

"Which is immaterial!" snapped Mrs. Nesbitt. "He sampled so much of the champagne he says is no good—probably from the bottles as well as the glasses—that he got staggering drunk!"

"No, ma'am," said Carter. "Jus' a few sips. An' only from the glasses. Like always. Some of us always taste the wine, but just what's left over in the glasses."

"But you were *drunk!*" Mrs. Nesbitt insisted. "You don't deny it, do you?"

"No, ma'am."

"And passed out. You don't deny you passed out?"

"No, ma'am. Twenty-three years, Ah—"

"There's the point," said Mrs. Roosevelt. "In twenty-three years, one transgression. We can't ask for saints for our employ. Let's give him another chance."

"Oh, Mrs. Roosevelt, Ah—"

Henrietta Nesbitt pointed menacingly at Sam Carter. "One chance, Sam," she said. "Just one and no more. Now get yourself into uniform and ready to work. I ought to demote you to a dishwasher."

Mrs. Roosevelt stared after the nervously retreating waiter. "Have you anything to tell me about Wednesday night?" she asked the housekeeper.

Mrs. Nesbitt shook her head. "It's hard to tell. They all swear they saw nothing. I have to wonder if they'd tell us if they did."

"None of the staff saw anyone, man or woman, come down to the bathrooms in the east end of the Ground-Floor halls? There is an open view from west to east."

"Our people going up to the butler's pantry use the west elevator mostly. Or the stairs. They are not even out into the hall. That our kitchen and waiting staff saw nothing proves nothing."

"People wander around here—"

"Excuse me. They don't. An officer was on duty at the east end of the hall."

"And did not see Senator Gibson come downstairs," said Gerald Baines. "I already identified the man and asked him."

"I doubt Senator Gibson ever came downstairs," said Mrs. Roosevelt. "Either he faked his illness and met someone in the East Room, or he never got farther than the East Room on his way down to the men's room."

"Kennelly will be here shortly," said Baines. "I think he has identified . . . Well, I shouldn't say identified. He has no names. But he has two unidentified suspects."

When Ed Kennelly arrived, Mrs. Roosevelt and Baines

were sitting in her study, over tea and some small sandwiches and pastries. They were silent, listening to the radio, which carried pessimistic news bulletins from France. Particularly dismaying were accounts of whole towns fleeing ahead of the advancing German armored divisions—and being strafed by an odd, ugly airplane the Germans had introduced into warfare during their campaign in Poland. Equipped with a shrill siren, the stuka—used chiefly as a dive bomber—was obviously meant to strike terror into the hearts of people who heard its menacing sound. The strafing of roads was not in fact causing wholesale casualties. It was achieving its purpose, however, which was to choke the roads with terrified civilians and impede the movement of Allied units.

"Terror . . ." said Mrs. Roosevelt quietly. "War is horrible. War is terrible. But am I wrong in thinking the intentional terrorizing of a civilian population is something new in man's inhumanity to man?"

"I was in France in 1917 and 1918," said Baines. "It has been a long time since civilians were spared the horrors of war."

"If in fact they *ever* were," said Kennelly.

"But was terror imposed on civilians accidentally, or intentionally?" asked Mrs. Roosevelt.

"Who can say?" asked Baines. "I can tell you one thing. It was imposed intentionally in France in my years there."

"The damned Germans—" said Kennelly.

Baines interrupted. "Germans, yes. I have family in Belgium and I am afraid of what—"

"Mr. Baines," Mrs. Roosevelt interrupted. "You have a family in Europe?"

"A sister," he said. "And her husband and children. My family name was DeBainville. God knows what will happen to them. But—I was about to say . . . Fearful as the Germans are, let's not forget the rape of Nanking. Forgive me, ma'am, but I *detest* the isolationists. Detest them! They have no sense of right and wrong."

"I should not wish to be quoted, Mr. Baines, Captain Kennelly," said the First Lady, "but I share your emotional commitment to the cause of humanity and decency."

"Senator Borah," said Baines sarcastically, "has the same morals in international affairs as he has in his own bed—which is to say, none. And it would be well for Charles Lindbergh to reflect on the fact that he is nothing but a reckless aviator who was foolish enough to take off on a flight he had no right to expect he would complete—which does not make him an expert on military aviation. I—I'm sorry. I have to think of my sister in Brussels."

Kennelly was more than a little discomfited by this exchange and kept looking back and forth between Baines and Mrs. Roosevelt. He kept his silence until they seemed finished, then said, "As an Irishman, I've no great love for the Brits—but I like them better than the murderin' Krauts, ye may be sure."

Baines was a little flushed. "Maybe we had better get back to what we came to talk about," he said.

Mrs. Roosevelt's sympathy went to Baines, but she doubted she could offer any comfort. "Yes," she said. "Captain—"

"Miss Tareytons and Miss Kools," he said, and he went on to explain to them about the two women who had apparently slept in the Georgetown apartment with Senator Gibson.

"What did your fingerprint men find?" asked the First Lady.

"Plenty of examples of the prints of Miss Tareytons—on the bathroom fixtures, bathroom glass, the headboard of the bed, and so on. But they do us no good, because the F.B.I. doesn't have any record of those fingerprints. There were some other smudged prints, again of no one the F.B.I.

has record of. We took prints from Lena and matched them to many prints found in the apartment."

"Amelia's?" asked Mrs. Roosevelt.

"That's interesting," said Kennelly. "The F.B.I. has her prints on record, as you know, but my boys found no prints of hers in the apartment."

Mrs. Roosevelt put the tip of her right index finger to the index finger of her left hand, as if to count. "So we know of four people who visited the Georgetown apartment: Senator Gibson himself, naturally, plus Miss Tareytons, Miss Kools, and Lena, the maid."

Kennelly nodded. "The neighbors were decidedly unfriendly toward police questions. They don't like the scandal of a murder touching their cozy lives in their cozy apartments. Three of them, all women, said they often saw the Senator going in and coming out. They saw Lena. None of them ever saw another woman enter or leave—including Mrs. Gibson."

"Amelia Gibson said she sometimes spent the night in their Georgetown apartment," said Mrs. Roosevelt.

"When she did, she found the place immaculate," said Kennelly. "No sign another woman had spent the last night there."

"We are not making assumptions, are we?" asked Mrs. Roosevelt.

"I'm curious about one thing," said Kennelly. "Lena said she never saw a woman at the apartment. The women who spent the night there left before she came in, usually around eight-thirty. If Mrs. Gibson spent nights there, why didn't Lena ever see her?"

"I am compelled," said Mrs. Roosevelt, "to ask a different question. How reliable a witness is Miss Lena Madison?"

"Mrs. Roosevelt," said Kennelly solemnly, "that young Negro woman is the most perceptive witness I ever talked to. She saw everything Jerry Baines and I had seen and reached the same conclusions."

The First Lady nodded. "Is there the remotest chance of a possibility, Captain Kennelly, that you saw what Miss Lena Madison wanted you to see? Is there any possibility that she arranged the apartment for you, before you came last evening? If the Senator were killed by—Well, if he were killed by representatives of the insurance industry, let us say, isn't it just remotely possible that they employed Miss Madison to create certain appearances for you?"

Kennelly smiled. "I complimented her," he said. "I told her she thought like Mrs. Roosevelt. Well . . . Maybe she does. Clever enough to cover up a murder. Clever enough to see the hole in the cover."

Aboard the presidential train returning to Washington, the President sat down with Harry Hopkins and reviewed advertisements in newspapers from New York and Washington. "Harry," he said, "war brings inflation. I suppose that is inevitable. Even a foreign war, to which we are not committed, brings inflation. I will be damned, though, if I can see why the war in Europe should bring the price of eggplant up to 10¢ a pound. *Eggplant,* Harry! I *like* eggplant. Will we need to impose price controls?"

Hopkins scanned the ads and read some of the prices— "Chuck steak 20¢ a pound, leg of lamb 25¢, spinach 4¢, cucumbers 7¢. On the other hand, the want ads are offering $20 a week for a typist-receptionist. Here's an ad for a bank clerk, $120 a month!"

"What's the word?" asked the President. " 'Spiral?' The trouble with spiraling wages and prices is that wages don't all spiral at the same rate. If a receptionist in some nice law or accounting firm can earn $20 a week, there are still plenty of dime-store clerks working for $8 a week, and 10¢ a pound for eggplant puts that vegetable beyond her means! The last thing in the world I want to do is suggest price controls. The Congress would never authorize them, in any case. But what's going to happen to the $8-a-week retail clerk? What's she supposed to eat, dandelion greens?"

"Nice flannel suit for $35," said Hopkins. "Think I'll duck out and buy one of those."

"What's a pair of bib overalls cost, Harry? That's the question."

"I don't know, Frank. When's the last time you ever bought a pair?"

"Don't be a smart aleck, Harry. They cost $1.55, the same as they did in 1932. And—"

Harry Hopkins laughed. "I wonder how many people in this country guess that Franklin D. Roosevelt knows the price of bib overalls!"

"Well . . . You and your $35 suit. A young lawyer can still go to his office, well togged out, in an $18.75 suit. When things like this get out of control, we are in deep trouble, Harry—and we'd better think of some way to sell price controls to the Congress and the public."

That evening Mrs. Roosevelt attended a dinner given in her honor by a group of congressional wives whose husbands were running for reelection. They hoped, probably, to obtain from her some hint of whether or not the President meant to run for a third term.

One of the congressional wives knew the answer. Claudia Johnson, known as "Lady Bird," knew that her husband had been working diligently to elect the Democratic National Convention a Texas delegation that would vote for Roosevelt on the first ballot. In this he was opposed even by his political mentor, Sam Rayburn, who supported Vice President Garner. She also knew that a compromise agreement had been reached and manifested in a telegram signed by her husband as leader of the Roosevelt faction and by Congressman Sam Rayburn as leader of the Garner faction. The Texas delegation would vote for Vice President Garner on the first ballot, so he would not be embarrassed. It would be a bow to old Cactus Jack, who would not be renominated for Vice President. President Roosevelt knew about the struggle and the compromise. He had not discouraged Congressman Lyndon Johnson from leading a third-term drive in Texas. Knowing this, Lady Bird Johnson knew with a high degree of certainty that the President would run.

But that night Mrs. Roosevelt did not know.

The Congressman brought Lady Bird Johnson to the dinner and stayed long enough to shake hands all around. He chatted for a few minutes with the First Lady and then quietly and respectfully asked her if she could give him a brief moment alone.

"It will have to be brief, Mr. Johnson. I—"

"Very brief, ma'am," said Johnson. "I want to give you a little piece of information about Senator Gibson."

Smiling at some of the other women and quietly excusing herself, she stepped a little way apart with the tall, gawky young Congressman Johnson.

He leaned over her. "Ma'am," he said, "I am sure you dislike gossip. So do I. In ordinary circumstances I wouldn't speak of what I'm about to speak of. But—"

"But the man was murdered," said Mrs. Roosevelt grimly.

"Yes. He surely was. Well . . . Wednesday night a young woman was rushed to the hospital in Georgetown. She had taken an overdose of sleeping pills. Fortunately, another young woman, who shared an apartment with her, found her and called an ambulance. She's still in the hospital in Georgetown. For a while they didn't think she'd make it, but she did."

"Who is this young woman?" asked Mrs. Roosevelt. "And what has this to do with Senator Gibson's murder?"

"Her name is Joanne Winthrop. What it has to do with Senator Gibson is that there has been gossip around for months that he and Miss Winthrop were having an affair.

She is from a very old Boston family, was a debutante and all that, and is supposed to be very beautiful."

"I know who she is," said the First Lady a little coldly.

"I'd hoped," said Johnson, "the story's not true. I wouldn't have mentioned it at all, except that she tried to kill herself within an hour or so after the Senator's death. The story was on every radio news broadcast that night, so it's likely she knew. Maybe it's a coincidence. I hope it is."

"Where did you hear the story, Mr. Johnson?"

"There's no place like Capitol Hill for gossip. The first time I heard it, I guess, was when I stopped in at Vice President Garner's office for a drink. Senator Gibson was there for the same reason, and when he left somebody sort of smiled after him and told the story. I've heard it several times since."

"I will try to initiate a . . . *discreet* inquiry into the subject," said Mrs. Roosevelt.

"I'm sorry to have to tell you," said Johnson gravely. "I genuinely don't like gossip."

V

On Saturday morning Mrs. Roosevelt was driven to a small white church in Manassas, Virginia, for the funeral of Senator Vance Gibson. She went as representative of the President. With her in the White House limousine were Secretary of State Cordell Hull and Senate Majority Floor Leader Alben Barkley. The morning was cool but juicy green, and a stiff breeze sent clouds sailing rapidly past the steeple of the little church.

Perhaps a hundred cars were parked along the road, bringing prominent people to the funeral. Twenty more senators were present, as well as at least as many members of the House of Representatives. Besides the Secretary of State, three more cabinet members were present, including Secretary of the Interior Harold Ickes. Way was made for the White House limousine to be drawn up to the front of the church. Unknown to Mrs. Roosevelt, the limousine bearing the widow had waited at a crossroads and had followed immediately behind the car from the White House.

Amelia Gibson came forward to seize the hand of the First Lady. "It is kind of you to come," she said.

The chubby little woman wore black. A heavy veil shadowed her face. She had been alone in her limousine. The Gibsons, as Mrs. Roosevelt now knew, had had no children. No one from Idaho had come. It would have been a burdensome train ride.

"Will you sit with me?" Amelia asked.

Mrs. Roosevelt nodded solemnly. "Of course," she said.

Hull and Barkeley were next to last to be escorted to their pew. A small gasp went up in the congregation when they saw that the widow was coming down the aisle on the arm of the nation's First Lady: a contrasting pair, Mrs. Roosevelt tall and spare, the little widow short and plump.

There was no casket.

Probably sensing Mrs. Roosevelt's puzzlement, Amelia looked up at her and whispered, "I had him cremated, as he wished."

Mrs. Roosevelt nodded noncommittally, though she herself could not imagine so disposing of the body of a loved one.

The service was Methodist. It was not protracted. When it was finished and they walked up the aisle again, Amelia said, "Will you come to the house? I've asked only a few people."

Mrs. Roosevelt suspected she would not have asked Cordell Hull and Alben Barkley, but they were in the White House limousine. At Fairlea it proved true that only a few people had been invited, mostly neighbors and social friends apparently, no more than half a dozen from Washington.

On the stone terrace behind the house, a bronze urn sat on one of the wrought-iron tables. Amelia picked it up by its two handles and spoke—

"Years ago Vance asked me . . . He asked me, if anything ever happened to him, to have his body cremated. He had a horror of being buried in the ground. He wanted his ashes scattered in one of the cold, tumbling streams in the Idaho mountains. When we came here and learned to love this place, he told me to pour his ashes into Bull Run. So now . . ." She paused, unable to go on. She put down the urn and used her fingers to wipe her eyes. Then— "Will you walk with me? I am going to carry his urn down to the stream and pour him on the water. Will all of you come with me?"

A small procession formed. Amelia leading, Mrs. Roosevelt beside her, they walked across the long meadow that sloped gently down to the little stream. The household staff and a tall white woman dressed in black watched from a respectful distance, then followed, keeping their distance. The First Lady wondered what role, if any, this meadow had played in the battle fought here almost eighty years ago. It was not part of the battlefield park, but it seemed likely that every acre of ground along both sides of Bull Run must have seen some action. She knew that bones, buckles, and bullets were still occasionally washed to the surface in a hard rainstorm and were collected from these fields.

They reached the bank of Bull Run. It was a small, quiet stream, a tributary of the Potomac.

Standing above the water on a point where the stream had undercut the bank and made an almost vertical boundary between field and water, Amelia unscrewed the cap of the urn. Almost before the others could assemble around her, she turned the urn upside down and let the ashes of her husband fall into Bull Run.

Mrs. Roosevelt realized to her horror that the contents were not just ashes but were also fragments of bone that rattled from the urn and dropped with small splashes on the green surface of the water. The fine gray ash drifted on the wind.

Amelia stood watching the ash drifting and falling to the water. Then—impulsively as it seemed to Mrs. Roosevelt— she cast the bronze urn and its lid into the stream.

*   *   *

Washington in 1940 was not a five-day-a-week town. No town was. For most Americans in that year the work week ended at noon on Saturday. Government offices, open eight to five weekdays, closed at noon on Saturday. On a fine June afternoon, thousands of office workers had not gone home but were in the parks, joined by their families, eating picnics, playing games, chasing after their children, or just lying in the sunlight, relaxing after a difficult week.

Not until mid-afternoon did the White House limousine bring the First Lady home. Amelia Gibson had served a buffet luncheon after she cast her husband's ashes on Bull Run. On the terrace, she had put aside her hat and veil and had chatted soberly but amiably with her guests.

No, she had said, she would not go back to Idaho. She had made a home here at Fairlea, and she meant to stay in it.

No, she had no idea who had killed her husband. It really made no difference, did it? Capturing his murderer would not bring him back to life.

No, she would not involve herself in Idaho politics. Her father had been regarded as a wild eccentric, and maybe she was, too, in a much smaller way.

She had been thinking since Wednesday evening about what she would do. A tour of Europe would have been nice but was now out of the question. Maybe a tour of South America—

Neither the Secret Service nor the homicide squad of the District police offered a five-day week either. When Mrs. Roosevelt returned to her study, she found a message saying that Gerald Baines and Captain Kennelly would see her at her convenience. Without changing out of the black clothes she had worn to the funeral, she called them to her study. They were in the White House and appeared within five minutes.

"We had no file on Joanne Winthrop," said Kennelly. "Neither did the F.B.I. No fingerprints—"

"She's not the kind of young woman who would be likely to be fingerprinted," said Baines.

"So we put together a file of our own, the best we could," Kennelly continued. "I like her picture."

They had obtained from one of the newspapers a glossy 8 × 10 print of a photograph taken at a charity ball a few months ago. Joanne Winthrop had been photographed sitting at a table with two other people—at least that was how many people appeared in the picture; likely others were around the table. The woman to the left in the picture was a bejeweled socialite, probably in her forties, not at all bad looking, smiling, and maybe a little self-conscious about her bare shoulders and her cleavage. The man in the middle was older, wearing a severely trimmed mustache, and a carnation in his buttonhole. Glasses and ashtrays occupied the foreground on the table.

Joanne Winthrop was turned away from the others, maybe to talk to someone else, more likely, from the look of her, because she was bored with whatever the others were saying. She was blond, though her eyebrows were dark. Her hair was carefully styled, exposing her ears, except for one managed curl. Her face had to be one of the most nearly perfect anyone had ever seen, flawed only, if at all, by a full lower lip that protruded a little, as if she were pouting. Her chin rested lightly in her left palm, and her left wrist was burdened with an obviously heavy gold bracelet, set with glittering gems. Her necklace was also heavy. In the black-and-white photograph the jewels of the necklace were light and dark, maybe diamonds and emeralds. Her shoulders were bare, and her cleavage was far deeper than that of the woman who seemed to be self-conscious about her own. If Joanne Winthrop was aware at all that her breasts were bare to the edges of her nipples, she conspicuously didn't care.

"Why would a young woman with that much beauty and poise have tried to take her own life?" asked Mrs. Roosevelt.

"Maybe because the newspapers have not been kind to her," said Kennelly.

The next item in the file was a clipping from the tabloid *Saturday Star*—

Postdeb Joanne Winthrop, seen last night at the Symphony Ball, continues to make a splash in Washington society. Working as an unpaid volunteer in the headquarters of American Red Cross, she lives as if there were no tomorrow, money-wise. For instance, we are reliably informed that the table she sponsored at the ball cost her $500.

Hurrah for Miss Winthrop! A mystery, however. Daddy—i.e., Mr. Gilford Winthrop of up Boston way— is reported to have sold his Cape Cod home because he could no longer afford to keep it up. Other evidences of a declining life style are reported by Boston papers. Sister Jennie married Endicott money and seems to have no problems. Brother Willie, on the other hand, is working, keeping the hours of a Stock Exchange clerk and living modestly, as is reported.

How is it that the beautiful, charming, poised Joanne continues to live in a style her parents and brother seem no longer able to afford? Rumors fly! Even the *Star* will not report what they are.

"Do you think she is Miss Tareytons?" asked Mrs. Roosevelt.

Kennelly shrugged. "I don't know. If she was, it's all but impossible that she could have killed him."

"Why?" asked Baines.

"Let's analyze that," said Mrs. Roosevelt. "First, the Senator's throat was cut. That took physical strength. Someone had to get behind him, perhaps pin his arms, then slit his throat with that razor. Second, Miss Winthrop was not in the White House last night—that is, she wasn't unless she entered like a burglar. Third, if she did kill Senator Gibson, why would she then go home and try to kill herself?"

"All right," said Kennelly. "None of that means she wasn't Miss Tareytons. None of it means she couldn't be a key to what happened."

"Granted," said Mrs. Roosevelt. "Our problem, really, is that we don't know what *motivated* someone to murder Senator Gibson."

"Could Miss Winthrop's father, or Miss Winthrop's brother have had a motive?"

"One of your words, my dear lady, that you've used in investigations before is 'fanciful,' " said Kennelly. "That's fanciful, isn't it? Isn't it?"

"Motive," said Baines. "We haven't looked at the only motive anyone has suggested—that someone in the insurance industry would rather have seen him dead than see his legislation pass. And that brings me to something else. We've been checking the people who sat at the many tables Wednesday night. I've got a list of people who ducked out during the evening. To go to the bathroom was the universal excuse. How do you like the name Howard McGinnis as a suspect?"

"Who's Howard McGinnis?" asked Kennelly.

"Congressman from Ohio," said Baines. "The joke on Capitol Hill is that the insurance companies claim a deduction for his depreciation on their income tax. Long-time insurance agent. Elected to the House in 1934. When the insurance companies say, 'Jump,' he asks 'How high?' "

Mrs. Roosevelt chuckled. "That's an old cliché, Mr. Baines."

"Let me tell you a little fraud he ran in Ohio," said Baines. "The state has maybe fifty thousand notaries public. Every one has to be bonded, and each one pays ten dollars a year premium on his bond. Guess how many dollars the insurance companies have laid out in the past ten years, paying for notary defalcations."

"Tell us," said Kennelly.

"Not one thin dime," said Baines. "Okay, ten dollars a year for each of fifty thousand notaries. Half a million a year in insurance premiums and that result in *no* claims. About a quarter of those bonds were written by the McGinnis Insurance Agency in Columbus—because of the McGinnis political connections. So . . . $125,000 a year in business that can't produce a claim. McGinnis took a twenty percent commission on that business. And that's only the beginning of it."

"One more example, Mr. Baines," said Mrs. Roosevelt.

"Bonds," said Baines. "All kinds of public officials are bonded. The premiums run high. Claims? Almost never. Little offices where ten thousand dollars cross the counter in a year are bonded for million-dollar losses."

"A lucrative business," said the First Lady.

"Very," said Baines. "Let me go through one more point. In 1928, McGinnis was summoned before a committee of the Ohio legislature and asked how much was collected in premiums on these bonds, against what in losses. You know how he answered? He refused to answer. And within a few days political pressure was put on the committee to make sure they didn't ask the question again."

"Senator Gibson . . . ?"

"Gibson's bill would require insurance companies to file reports, comparing claims paid to premiums collected. They'd rather kill than make such reports. The fraud is nationwide, not just an Ohio case. Hundreds of millions of dollars are involved."

"You have been working hard, Mr. Baines," said the First Lady.

"No, ma'am. All I did was spend an hour and a half interviewing a member of Senator Gibson's staff. The young woman told me she wasn't surprised the Senator was murdered. She had feared it and had warned the Senator."

"And I suppose McGinnis was here Wednesday night," said Kennelly.

"As a matter of fact, he wasn't," said Baines. "That is, he wasn't in the State Dining Room. But a friend of his was. Do you recognize the name Hugh Emmett?"

"Senator from Alabama," said Mrs. Roosevelt.

"He left his table and went to the men's room about the time when Senator Gibson did," said Baines.

"All right, but how does that relate to McGinnis?" asked Kennelly.

"It is possible," said Baines, "that Senator Emmett let McGinnis in. Then McGinnis—"

"Now wait a minute," Kennelly interrupted. "Why could Senator Emmett let—"

"Because Senator Emmett, who is more than seventy years old and is retiring—which is why he was at the dinner—is not the strong man it must have taken to kill Senator Gibson. But Congressman McGinnis is. Senator Emmett is the chief opponent in the Senate of the Gibson Bill. He has spoken violently against it."

"Really, Mr. Baines, isn't this farfetched?"

"It might be, except for one thing," said Baines. "The staff member checked the criminal records of these two men. Senator Emmett has none. He comes from a small town in Alabama, where everybody knows everything about everybody else. Howard McGinnis is from Cleveland. In 1921 he was arrested, convicted, and sentenced to six months in jail . . . for attacking a man with a razor. A thing like that is forgotten in a city like Cleveland. Anyway, he moved down to Columbus. When he ran for Congress, no one brought it up against him."

"The staff girl told you this?" asked Mrs. Roosevelt.

"She feared it," he said. "She'd picked up most of the information over the last six months. She's done nothing since Wednesday night but track information of this kind."

"Who is this young woman?"

"Her name is Laura Mason. She worked her way through law school here in Washington and will take the bar examination this summer. She went to work in Senator Gibson's office as a secretary. She was a legislative assistant until Wednesday evening."

"I'm afraid I have to ask a question," said Mrs. Roosevelt. "Did you notice whether or not this young woman smokes cigarettes?"

Baines nodded. "Yes, she does."

"Ah. And what brand does she smoke?"

"I really wish I hadn't noticed and you hadn't asked," said Baines. "She smokes Kools."

Kennelly showed his badge to the young woman who opened the door to the apartment. "I'm Captain Edward Kennelly, D.C. police. I'd like to speak with Miss Winthrop," he said. "Is that possible?"

The young woman regarded him gravely, hesitantly for a moment, then said, "I suppose it's *possible;* but I don't think it's a very good idea. She's still very weak, and she's sleeping right now."

"Your name would be Miss Brenda Frelinghuysen," he said.

She nodded. She was a slight young woman, dark-haired, with a distinctive little face: pointed nose, pointed chin, thin mouth, intense dark eyes—on the whole, not conventionally beautiful, yet singularly appealing. "I don't think I want to know how you come to have my name," she said.

"Nothing ominous," he said. "Can I come in? Maybe *you* can talk to me for a minute or so."

"I can hardly say no," she said. "Come in. Sit down. I was having a Scotch and soda when the doorbell rang. Would you like one?"

"Thank you, yes," said Kennelly.

She smiled slyly at him. "It's only a legend, then, that policemen don't drink on duty."

"The legend doesn't apply to Irish cops."

She laughed. She stepped into the doorway toward the rear of the apartment and spoke to someone who was apparently in the kitchen. "Lena, will you bring a Scotch and soda, please?"

The apartment that Brenda Frelinghuysen shared with Joanne Winthrop was small but luxuriously furnished, as Kennelly judged it. A love seat and two chairs were upholstered with striped silk in bright warm colors. Three handsome paintings hung from the walls, each with its own little light attached to its frame. He guessed they were French.

Brenda Frelinghuysen was dressed in loose white silk pajamas. He had heard the phrase "hostess pajamas" and guessed that was what she was wearing. She lit a cigarette. Chesterfields.

"I imagine there is some purpose for this visit," she said.

"Oh, yes. When a person attempts to commit suicide, we have to look into it. The hospital has to report it; then we have to complete the file."

"What do you need to know?"

"Why she did it."

"Well, I don't know," said Brenda Frelinghuysen, putting her cigarette aside in an ashtray and lifting her glass. "And I suspect she doesn't know either, exactly."

"Did she ever try it before?"

"Not that I ever heard of. We've lived together here for about eight months, and she never tried it during that time. To the contrary. I thought she was happy."

"What does she live on, Miss Frelinghuysen?"

"I don't know exactly. I believe her father sends her an allowance."

"It must be a rather generous allowance," Kennelly suggested. "Have you seen the newspaper stories to the effect that her father is having financial difficulties?"

Brenda Frelinghuysen did not answer immediately. She waited while the maid came in with the Scotch and soda she had ordered for Kennelly. The maid was Lena Madison, the young black woman who had been the maid in the Gibson apartment also. She gave no sign she recognized Kennelly, and he gave no sign he recognized her. When she left the room, Brenda Frelinghuysen continued the conversation.

"Joanne told me about them. She said they are not true. All I can tell you about that is that she pays her half of the rent here. She has money for clothes and entertainment and for her charities."

"How long has she lived with you?"

"About eight months. Before that she had an apartment in The Willows. You know . . . the apartment hotel."

Kennelly drew a deep breath and pondered his next question. To gain a moment to think, he sipped from his Scotch. "The questions necessarily become somewhat personal," he said.

"I thought they were already somewhat personal," said she.

"Not nearly as personal as they are about to get. And I'm sorry I have to ask questions like this."

"If you're sorry, why do you?"

He sighed loudly. "I'm not just investigating a suicide attempt, Miss Frelinghuysen. I'm investigating something a great deal more serious."

"I suspected that," she said, picking up her cigarette and dragging on it.

"I have to ask this question. Does Miss Winthrop sleep in this apartment every night?"

Brenda Frelinghuysen drummed her fingers on the leather-topped table in front of her love seat. "A detective . . . A *captain.* Investigating something a great deal more serious . . . I suppose I have to hear these questions."

"You have to answer them," said Kennelly.

She nodded. "The answer is no. She stays away over-night, two or three nights a week. On the average."

"Do you know where? With whom?"

She shook her head.

"Let me guess," he said. "When she stays away overnight, she comes home very early in the morning. Maybe seven o'clock. Maybe earlier."

"If you know all that, why are you asking me these questions? I guess you know more than I do."

"Let me guess something else. She smokes Herbert Tareyton cigarettes."

Brenda Frelinghuysen's face darkened. "What do you suspect her of doing, Captain Kennelly. You're investigating a murder, aren't you? Can you possibly suspect Joanne is guilty of *murder?*"

"No. No, I assure you I don't suspect her of murder," he said. "To the contrary, I think she may be a victim of the murder I'm investigating."

"Victim . . . ? But she's alive!"

"Help me with something, Miss Frelinghuysen," said Kennelly. "Speak frankly. In complete confidence. Whatever answer you give me to my next two or three questions, I will not repeat what you tell me. Not anywhere. Not to anyone."

"You're asking me to trust you?"

He nodded. "May I assume that Miss Winthrop is not the kind of girl who . . . Who just sleeps around. May I assume that?"

Brenda Frelinghuysen nodded. "I think Joanne has a very good set of morals."

"That being the case, she was not absent from this apartment two or three nights a week, just sleeping around," said Kennelly. "It is likely, then, that she was in love with someone, isn't it?"

"*Was?*"

"She attempted suicide because the man she loved was murdered," said Kennelly.

"My god! You're talking about Senator Gibson!"

Kennelly nodded. "He was murdered Wednesday evening. It was on the radio news within half an hour. She heard it—"

"And tried to kill herself . . ."

"The facts go together that way, don't they?"

"Captain Kennelly . . . Joanne is the most beautiful, intelligent, caring girl in the world. She grew up in opulence. She was a debutante of the Silver Rose—that is, in Vienna. Then, in Boston, something happened to her. I don't know the details. An unhappy love affair, followed by humiliation. She wanted to get away from Boston. Her father wouldn't support her with an allowance if she chose to live in New York. So it was Philadelphia or Washington—or maybe Baltimore. She chose to come to Washington, to enter into an entirely different milieu."

"Washington is different from Boston," said Kennelly dryly.

"Yes. Captain Kennelly, you have to understand what Joanne offers to the man she marries. Elegance. Grace. That's her life. That's what she was educated to do: to run a beautiful home with style and refinement."

"Assuming she was in fact involved in a love affair with Senator Vance Gibson, how did that offer her the chance to run a beautiful home? The Senator was married."

Brenda Frelinghuysen shook her head. "I don't have an answer for that. Maybe she was stupid enough to fall in love with him."

"Not only was he married," said Kennelly. "The money that made it possible for him to live in style was his wife's."

Brenda smiled. "Have you ever seen that grotesque little woman? Daughter of a silver miner. A *parvenu,* Captain, if you know what the word means. *Nouveau riche.* A pretender after elegance. She is a paradigm of bad taste."

"I wouldn't know about that, Miss Frelinghuysen. Myself, I'm lace-curtain Irish."

"My family, Captain, are solid Dutch burghers, six or eight generations removed from Netherlands mud. I suppose we've acquired a certain style, but—"

"It's a high privilege to be able to mock your own family," said Kennelly.

"The Winthrops don't mock theirs, I may tell you," she said.

"Can we hold this conversation entirely in confidence, Miss Frelinghuysen? I mean to the extent that you don't even tell Miss Winthrop I was here."

"You assure me she is not a suspect?"

"Not in the least. Considering when the murder happened and how it happened— Uh . . . Incidentally, can you tell me where *you* were Wednesday evening?"

She laughed. "Playing bridge," she said. "I've got seven alibi witnesses."

"Then I am going to tell you something that may be a little helpful to you in trying to help Miss Winthrop," said Kennelly. "I left in my car a copy of the report written by the doctors who treated her at Georgetown University Hospital. I'll keep your secret. You keep mine."

"Agreed."

Kennelly picked up his glass and stared for a moment at the bit of Scotch left in it. "When Miss Winthrop was brought in unconscious, they doubted she would survive—"

"It was lucky I got home when I did."

"Yes. What she had taken had nearly killed her. It had also done something else, Miss Frelinghuysen. It caused her to miscarry. She lost a two-month fetus during the night."

"Abortion . . . ?" Brenda whispered.

He shook his head. "No. I'm satisfied she meant to kill herself, not specifically the baby—though it would have of course died with her. I think she did it because she'd just heard the baby's father had been killed."

VI

On Sunday the President received a cable from Paul Reynaud, Premier of France—

TODAY THE ENEMY IS ALMOST AT THE GATES OF PARIS. A PORTION OF THE GOVERNMENT HAS ALREADY LEFT PARIS. I AM MAKING READY TO LEAVE FOR THE FRONT. WE SHALL CONTINUE THE FIGHT, AND IT IS MY DUTY TO ASK YOU FOR NEW AND EVEN LARGER ASSISTANCE.

The President cabled Winston Churchill and asked how long Paris could hold out. Paris would probably be occupied tomorrow, Churchill replied—though the Germans might choose not to make an all-out assault but to surround the city and wait until they could enter unresisted.

There was one glimmer of good news. The French had withdrawn virtually all their forces from southern France in order to meet the German blitz in the north. Only five French divisions remained to face the thirty-two Italian divisions Mussolini had thrown into his invasion. Five proved enough. They stopped the Italian army cold.

United States Ambassador to France William Bullit ca-

77

bled that the French army was fighting with magnificent courage, "determined to make the fall of France as magnificent as her past." Churchill, though, forwarded to the President an eyewitness account of the situation in and around Paris, sent to London by a Reuters correspondent. It described the French army as utterly routed, "drifting aimlessly into Paris and on through to the south, most of the soldiers drunk, having abandoned their rifles."

The plight of the refugees on the roads south of the city was indescribable. Many of them were attacking local people to obtain drinking water.

The First Lady had gone to church and from there to a picnic afternoon in Anacostia Park, organized by the International Ladies Garment Workers Union. Alone in his study, the President read the newspapers and the cables, listened to the radio news, and worked on his stamp collection. He was despondent, burdened by the frustrating feeling that even if he could persuade the Congress and the nation to do more for Western Civilization, nothing they could do at this hour would save France—and maybe save Britain.

Missy had gone to Mass and had eaten her lunch alone in her suite. Sensing that the President would be depressed by the awful news coming in from France, she went to him in his study late in the afternoon. He welcomed her, handed her a magnifying glass, and began an animated description of why two apparently identical stamps were not identical and why one was worth ten cents and the other fifty dollars.

In Anacostia Park, Mrs. Roosevelt strolled among women, chiefly—but many men, too—who had come out for the ILGW picnic. The sun shone brightly on their outing. Almost all the men had shed their jackets and greeted the sun in shirtsleeves. The women wore white or pastel prints. Children dashed around barefoot.

Two softball games had been organized, as had been sack races and one-legged races: picnic games in which people pulled heavy potato sacks up over their legs and hopped wildly on a fifty-yard course, or tied the right leg of one partner to the left of the other and struggled to run the course that way. Stakes for horseshoe pitching had been driven, and enthusiastic crowds watched those games.

Two men were kept busy squeezing lemons for great crocks of lemonade. Hotdogs sizzled on the grills in stone fireplaces. Tables were heaped with platters of sliced tomatoes and cucumbers. Bowls of baked beans and potato salad sat heavily on the same tables. Open jars offered an endless variety of pickles: dill, sweet, Polish, kosher, bread-and-butter, and so on, plus relishes of all colors.

Besides the First Lady, many political people were there. Frances Perkins, Secretary of Labor, Henry Wallace, Secretary of Agriculture, Vice President and Mrs. Garner, many members of Congress and their wives, plus even a few officers from Fort McNair and the Navy Yard.

The picnickers were leaders of labor, and most of them were well informed and aware. They talked to her about the third term and about who might be nominated to run for Vice President if the President ran again. They talked about the developing baseball season. They talked about the upcoming heavyweight match between Joe Louis and Arturo Godoy, and some expressed the opinion that at last the Bronx Bomber had met his match. Godoy had boxed Louis fifteen rounds in February, and he had learned his weaknesses and would put him away this time. The Republicans, some said, had no chance in November—provided the President ran. They cited the old political adage, "You can't beat somebody with nobody."

None of them, absolutely none, said anything about the war in Europe. It was as if the Germans were not forty miles from Paris. Mrs. Roosevelt wondered what really mattered to them.

The Gibson murder did. A dozen or more people raised the subject when she talked with them. A reporter from the Washington *Post* asked—

"Bob Kimmel of the *Post,* Mrs. Roosevelt. Has there been any break in the investigation of the murder of Senator Gibson?"

"Not that I am aware of, Mr. Kimmel. You would know more readily than I."

The reporter grinned. "There have been rumors that you take a personal hand in investigating a very special case now and again. There was a story, for example, that you had a hand in solving the mystery surrounding the death of Ambassador Troyanoski on the liner *Normandie* in 1938. It's been said that you contributed a lot to solving the mystery surrounding the murder of Philip Garber last year."

She smiled at him. "I imagine you understand, young man," she said, "that if you believe ten percent of what some people say about me, you will have believed ten percent too much."

"But this murder happened in the White House!"

"There have been other crimes in the White House," she said calmly. "Congressman Colmer was shot to death in the Oval Office itself in 1934. I did contribute a small something to the solution of that mystery, by pointing out how the door could have been latched from outside. That was a locked-room mystery, Mr. Kimmel. But the solution was simple. Believe me, if any special insights come to me that might help solve the mystery surrounding the tragic death of Senator Gibson, I will communicate them immediately and directly to the police."

"The crime is four days old!"

"That proves only one thing," she said.

"What?"

"That you can count, young man. That you can count."

* * *

Baines was married. Kennelly was not. Both men would have worked Sunday, but neither of them saw anything they could profitably do. The people they wanted to see were not easy to find on Sunday. Washington was not a five-day-a-week town, but it surely was a six-day-a-week town. People resented being disturbed on what was for them either their sabbath or their day of rest.

Baines stayed at home with his family, listening to the news, alert to any mention of Brussels. Kennelly slept late, took a blueplate meal in a downtown restaurant, and went to a late-afternoon movie. He would have enjoyed the show at the Gaiety Burlesque, but that was closed on Sunday.

In her study on Monday morning, Mrs. Roosevelt received a telephone call from Amelia Gibson—

"Oh, Mrs. Roosevelt, it was so kind of you to come Saturday! I hope I am not imposing, but I would so much enjoy seeing you in happier circumstances. Greta Garbo is arriving tomorrow morning. She's a friend, as you may know, and she's going to stay with me for a week or so. I thought you might like to meet her. She's a little standoffish, as you've probably heard. I have to promise her she won't be deviled by friends and neighbors—and *particularly* by reporters. When I told her on the phone that *you* might come, she told me to ask you, by all means."

"When would you like me to come, dear?"

"Could you come for lunch? Oh, could you?"

The First Lady glanced at her desk calendar. Lunch at Fairlea tomorrow would require some adjustment of her schedule, but she did not want to disappoint poor Amelia Gibson. "I shall be there at twelve, if that's what you have in mind."

"You are so kind."

*   *   *

"There is no question in my mind," said Kennelly. "Joanne Winthrop is Miss Tareytons. She tried to kill herself because she had lost the man she loved. I feel sorry for her."

"Obviously, then, she is not a suspect," said Mrs. Roosevelt. "She could not have killed him because he'd told her that afternoon that he was casting her aside, maybe going back to his wife. Even if that were possible, which I am convinced it is not, why would she then go home and try to kill herself?"

"I am entirely convinced she is not the murderer," said Kennelly.

"Unless she hired someone to do it," Baines suggested. "Or allied herself with someone who did it."

"I think we had better focus our attention on someone else," said Mrs. Roosevelt. "Of course . . . Of course, I offer that only as a suggestion. *I* am not in charge of the investigation. It is good to have identified Miss Tareytons. I would like to know who Miss Kools was, also. Do you think that was Miss Mason?"

"If it was," said Baines, "she may have been in his apartment as a legislative assistant, not as—"

"According to Lena," Kennelly interrupted, "Miss Tareytons did not wear perfume, leaving its odor on the bedclothes. Miss Kools did. Not conclusive evidence, but I think it does suggest that Miss Kools slept with the Senator, too."

"Then maybe Miss Kools had motive to kill him," said Mrs. Roosevelt. "But once again, that is a woman who would not have had access to the White House Wednesday evening."

"I want to go after the insurance thing," said Kennelly. "I think Laura Mason told Jerry the truth, but I'd like to see her, confront her with the fact that we have some evidence she slept with Gibson, and—"

"You have some fingerprints for Miss Kools, have you not?"

"Well . . . Some smudged samples. Not very good ones."

"Good enough to eliminate Miss Mason as Miss Kools— even if not good enough to positively identify her as such?"

"Good enough for that, probably."

"Let's arrange a meeting with Miss Mason."

"What about Congressman McGinnis and Senator Emmett?" asked Baines.

"We are going to have to leave that to Captain Kennelly," said Mrs. Roosevelt. "The political implications of *my* suggesting that one or both of them is guilty of murder are too great to contemplate. A southern Democrat and an Ohio Republican. I shudder."

As soon as Captain Edward Kennelly was comfortably seated on a couch in his Senate office, Senator Hugh Emmett produced a bottle of bourbon and two glasses.

"Little sip of bourbon between two gentlemen?" he asked, apparently deferentially.

"If you're drinkin' too, Senator," said Kennelly. "Never let it be said an Irishman passed up the chance to take a sip—though, I ask you, do you favor the delicacy that comes out of our Irish pot stills?"

Senator Emmett smiled as he poured. "I favor what comes out of *any* stills, sir. I remember my daddy sayin' to me one hot, dry summer, 'Son, don't buy no whisky this summer. It's got so dry they're usin' the *green* water out'n hog wallers.' I do favor it to be a little dark in color. The clear stuff, out'n Mason jars, can damage a man's voice."

Kennelly laughed. Genuinely, he laughed. The Senator was elderly and slight. He didn't seem to fill his suit. His face was pallid. His hands trembled a little. He was, even so—as Kennelly's little research on him had shown—still a man of firm opinions and significant influence. A lifelong lawyer, a one-time judge, he was a member of the Senate Judiciary Committee. He was credited with playing a major role in defeating the antilynching bill that failed in Congress in 1935. He was retiring now, but he had been a leader of the coalition of southern Democrats who had blocked, by filibuster and otherwise, every effort to legislate rights for blacks.

The N.R.A. codes, for example, had set lower standards for pay for black workers than white. Debating that issue on the floor of the Senate, Emmett had made a statement that would always be associated with his name—

"Y' listenin' to a man that was rocked in his cradle by a nigger, that was taught to fish by a nigger, that's always had niggers workin' in his own house, trusted to raise his own children th' way his mother trusted 'em to raise *him*. Y' listenin' to a man that sat by a nigger mammy's bed and held her hand when she died, then paid for a first-class funeral for her, 'cause she'd earned it. Man that give her children money to he'p 'em get a start in life. You from the No'th, you wanta tell *me* I hate niggers? Shoot, y' don't *know* no niggers your own selves, an' y' don't know what y' talkin' 'bout."

Senator Emmett sipped bourbon, then said, "I know why y' come to see me. Well, I can't he'p y' none. It's true I left my table at the White House and went to the men's room, 'bout the same time I guess that Senator Gibson left his and started out for the same place. Man my age has to go more often than a man his age. So I went. But I didn't see him."

Kennelly nodded. "What's hard in this investigation is to find a motive," he said.

"Why'd a man wanta kill Senator Gibson? I'm damned 'f I know, Captain. There are *those*, in the Senate and other places, disliked Senator Gibson fiercely. They shouldn't, but they did. Myself, I can't think of a single issue where him and me might of voted the same way." He paused and smiled. "Oh, on th' record, I'm sure we did. But he and I were men of very different *views.* The Senate, the Congress, is a place where men of different views get together and negotiate and compromise, and out of that process comes good things."

Kennelly took a drink of Scotch and tried to decide what to ask next—if anything. Senator Hugh Emmett was either a semisenile innocent, mouthing clichés, or an egregious liar. Kennelly decided to talk specifics.

"It's been suggested some in the insurance industry might have wanted to kill him," he said.

Senator Emmett nodded. "If anybody had reason to want him dead, the insurance boys would. His bill would have been very bad for the industry."

"You opposed it."

"Damn right," said Senator Emmett. "Generally, I oppose any legislation that wants to set up some kind of gov'ment control over any segment of business and th' economy. Gov'ment can foul up *anythin',* Captain. Y' ever read, like, Voltaire, Locke, Montesquieu, Diderot, Adam Smith? Them? They taught us gov'ment spends too much money. Always. Every time. Why? 'Cause they spendin' *other* folks' money. 'That gov'ment is best that governs least.' Oh, yes. Jefferson. Patrick Henry. Sam Adams. How'd *them* old fellas think about loadin' down th' insurance industry with a load of federal regulations."

"I know you understand, Senator, that I didn't come here to suggest you had anything at all to do with the death of Senator Gibson," said Kennelly. "I came to ask if you'd seen anything in the halls of the White House Wednesday night. I came to ask if you have any idea who might have hated the Senator and his bill so much that they'd kill him to stop him."

"Y' have my answer to the first question," said Senator Emmett. "I saw nothin'. As to the second . . . Sure, there could be men in th' insurance business that would kill to stop the Gibson Bill. It'd cost th' industry hundreds of millions of dollars. Who? Well, sir. You'd have to find a man who was in the White House Wednesday night. I was there, and I didn't see anybody I thought didn't have no business bein' there. I'm afraid I can't help you any more than that."

"One other question, Senator," said Kennelly. "There are rumors—I am told a lot of rumors—circulating on Capitol Hill to the effect that Senator Gibson was seeing a woman other than his wife. Would you want to comment on that?"

"Difference between you an' me, Captain Kennelly," said Senator Emmett. "You a No'therner, Washin'tonian anyway. Y' know . . . in th' South a man could get horsewhipped for askin' a question like that."

"And good for the South," said Kennelly. "But I have to investigate a murder. A senator is dead. Questions I'd be ashamed to ask in other circumstances—"

"True for you, Captain. You gotta point. You a gent'man who wouldn't ask if you didn't have your certain obligation. Right?"

"Right."

"Well . . . I s'pose there's not many men on Capitol Hill don't enjoy life in various ways. You a good-lookin' young man like Vance Gibson, you can cut a pretty wide swath. I'd say he cut a wide one, all I hear. And don' feel too sorry 'bout his wife. 'Cause the story goin' 'round for a long time is that she cuts some didoes of her own."

"That's an interesting point, Senator. What more can you say about that?"

"Western girl from Idaho. Her daddy was a hard-drinkin', hard ridin'—an' when I say ridin' I mean somethin' but horses—man that made more money than he knew what to do with. McCabe was his name. Irishman like you, I reckon. Story is, his daughter is a chip off th' ole block."

"Not just gossip?" asked Kennelly.

"Who knows?" Senator Emmett answered with a shrug. "Washin'ton's a awful place for gossip. Not much to do here, 'specially summers, but to trade scandalous stories.

'Fore Roosevelt, we went home summers. Now we sit around in the heat, drink more'n we oughta, and trade stories 'bout each other. Well, the Gibsons gave us many an entertainin' evenin'."

"Another name has come up in the course of the investigation," said Kennelly. "Can I mention it in confidence?"

"Co'se. What name?"

"Congressman Howard McGinnis."

"If we're talkin' in confidence, I'll say that Howard McGinnis is no gent'man. He's about as low a snake as there is in Congress. I opposed Senator Gibson's insurance bill, but I could respect the man. McGinnis agreed with me on the Gibson Bill—and on other issues besides—but I couldn't respect him."

Laura Mason received Ed Kennelly in her apartment on West Virginia Avenue. "Police . . ." she said. "I gave my suspicions to the man from the Secret Service. What more can I say?"

Kennelly faced a compact young woman, maybe twenty-five years old—red hair cut short, freckled pallid face, a solid womanly figure. She lived in a modest apartment that did not look permanent. She was modestly dressed: modestly, that is, in that she was well covered in a white cotton blouse and black skirt, but also in that what she wore was conspicuously modest in price. He noticed also that she was wearing some sort of musty-smelling perfume. He was no judge of perfume, but he guessed it was the most expensive thing she was wearing.

"Answer this question," said Kennelly. "Will you give me your fingerprints?"

"I will if you answer *my* question," she said. "Why do you *want* my fingerprints? Where do you think you've seen them?"

"In Senator Gibson's apartment."

Laura Mason nodded. "Okay. Granted. You found my fingerprints in Senator Gibson's apartment. What is the significance of that?"

"You worked for the Senator. You went to his apartment on business," said Kennelly.

"So?"

"Did you work in the bedroom? Fingerprints that may be yours were found there. You smoke Kools, don't you? His maid found Kools butts in the bedroom ashtray."

Kennelly was exaggerating a little. Lena Madison had not specifically said she'd found Kools butts in the bedroom. Sometimes, though, it was a good tactic to go beyond what you actually knew.

Laura sighed. "Okay. Vance and I . . . Hey! He was a wonderful man! Who killed him, for god's sake? Who—?"

"You have some firm ideas about that," said Kennelly.

"I guess you're not suggesting *I* killed him."

Kennelly shook his head. "No. I guess, though, you may know something more than you told Jerry Baines."

Laura Mason shrugged. She shook a cigarette out of a package of Kools, lit it, and said, "You ask the questions. I'll give the answers."

"Let's get something out of the way," he said. "You had an intimate relationship with Senator Gibson. Right?"

Laura Mason nodded. "I'd be some kind of fool to deny it."

"For a long time, several months anyway, you were . . . How do I say it? His chief woman? I mean, he was married, but you were sleeping two or three nights a week in his apartment. Right?"

She sighed. "Right."

"But after awhile you found out that somebody else was sleeping with him, too. Right?"

She smiled and shook her head. "After awhile I found it out? Hell, Captain. You don't know anything about Vance

Gibson. There was never a time when I was the only woman sleeping with Vance Gibson."

"Uh . . . What does that make you, Miss Mason?"

"It makes me a whore, Captain Kennelly. I had a job with him, which I got because he saw he could sleep with me. He would ordinarily have hired a girl from Idaho to work for him. Right? Isn't that how senators staff their offices: with people from their home states? You heard about Hollywood casting couches? I laid down on Vance's couch the first time I met him. And, what the hell, I'd have done the same in the office of just about any senator. So it was no big deal for me. It was what I expected. I decided a long time ago, Captain Kennelly, I'd do whatever I had to do to get where I'm going—which is, I'm going to be a *lawyer*. I did it with Vance Gibson, and—"

"There was a little more to it than that, wasn't there, Miss Mason?"

"Sure . . ."

"You fell in love with him, didn't you?"

Laura Mason nodded. "Every woman who ever knew him fell in love with him," she said. "I was just one of . . . Hell. Men liked him, too. I don't mean intimately. What I mean is, I don't think I ever met anyone who didn't like Vance Gibson. *Everybody* liked him. And a lot of women loved him."

"Mrs. Gibson . . . ?" asked Kennelly soberly.

Laura Mason sucked smoke from her Kool and put it aside. "I met her a couple of times. I sensed she understood that I was not just Vance's loyal employee. I *sensed* it. What good is that? I could be wrong. I— Hell, Captain, what do I know? I had the idea that she knew and didn't care. I could be so wrong it . . . I could be very, very wrong. Maybe I was trying to rationalize."

"Someone else took your place in the last few months," said Kennelly.

"Took my place? No. I never *had* a place."

"Did you love him?"

She closed her eyes and nodded. "I sure did. But I was realistic. I knew I could never have him. It would've been like sleeping with F.D.R. You might have him for the night, but you could never have him for life. You understand what I mean?"

"But you knew someone else had moved in."

She nodded. "Sure. You didn't have to be a wizard to figure out that."

"Who?"

"I didn't know. I don't know."

"Miss Mason, I have to ask you an awkward question. But I'm investigating a murder, and I'm going to ask it. Did the Senator ever give you money?"

Laura Mason stared at him for a moment, grim and somber; then she grinned and laughed. "Of *course* he gave me money. He gave me a job, and he gave me money. I mean, he gave me money besides what I was paid to work for him. That's how I knew he didn't love me. Listen, Captain. I never for a moment suggested he leave his wife and marry me. I knew he wouldn't. And I imagine that was what kept him with me as long as it was."

"You've laid some heavy accusations against the insurance industry," said Kennelly. "Against specific people."

She nodded.

"Why?"

She nodded again. "He was a *dear* man. More than that, I happen to think he might have become the Democratic candidate for President. Not this year, of course, or maybe not even in 1944; but he was a young man with a brilliant future ahead of him. I goddamn *resent* his death. Captain Kennelly . . . Suppose he'd tossed me aside. Suppose he didn't take me to the White House as a member of his staff. I'd still have been a woman who'd slept with the President of the United States. How many women can say that?"

"Let's talk about Howard McGinnis," said Kennelly. "You

gave Baines a complete rundown on him. How'd you get all that information?"

"Senator Gibson assigned me to find out all I could about Congressman McGinnis, months ago. He disliked him intensely. The Congressman returned the favor."

"He thought McGinnis was a crook?"

"Right. He expected McGinnis would lead the House fight against the Gibson Bill. More than that, he figured McGinnis would tell lies, pay bribes, or do anything else he thought might work. The Senator wanted ammunition he could use to discredit McGinnis."

"And you found some."

"It took a little doing, but I found a lot. McGinnis found out about it eventually. He confronted me in a hall one day and raised hell. He called me a cheap little snoop and warned me to lay off. I told him he'd have to talk to the Senator, that I was only doing what the Senator ordered. He stormed into the office and confronted the Senator. Senator Gibson threw him out of the office. I mean literally. He grabbed him by the seat of the pants and the nape of the neck and gave him the bum's rush."

"When was that?"

"A month or so ago."

"Are you saying you think McGinnis murdered the Senator?"

"He's the only man I can think of who might have. But he wasn't at the White House dinner. He'd have had to get in some way. That's your department. He's a vicious man, capable of murder I'm sure. But if he didn't have the opportunity—" She shrugged unhappily.

"So," said Mrs. Roosevelt when she met at the end of the day with Kennelly and Baines. "We can be confident we have identified Miss Tareytons and Miss Kools: Miss Winthrop and Miss Mason. I'm not sure it does us any good, but at least we know."

"I suppose I'm going to have to confront McGinnis," said Kennelly.

"I'm not certain I would, if you don't mind a suggestion. If we cannot place him in the White House last Wednesday evening, I cannot see how he could be the guilty party."

"How could he have known when Senator Gibson would leave the dining room?" asked Kennelly, nodding his agreement with the First Lady.

"How could he have known the Senator would leave the dining room at all?" she asked.

"McGinnis hated Senator Gibson," said Kennelly. "Unless Laura Mason is lying, which will be easy enough to check out, he hated the Senator. But if he killed him, he must have had help. Someone inside the White House that evening—"

"The Senator," said Mrs. Roosevelt, "left the State Dining Room because he was ill, nauseous. Unfortunately, the cause of death was so obvious there was no autopsy."

"The body could be exhumed," suggested Baines.

"Not this body, Mr. Baines," said Mrs. Roosevelt. "It was cremated and the ashes scattered on Bull Run."

VII

Mrs. Roosevelt left the White House not long after eleven, for her drive to Fairlea. Lately the Secret Service had begun firmly to insist that she had to take an agent along with her. She did not take Baines. She was accompanied by Dominic Deconcini, a young agent.

At Fairlea she found that Amelia Gibson had put aside her black mourning clothes and received her on the terrace in a light yellow spring frock. On the terrace too was the exquisitely beautiful Swedish actress, Greta Garbo.

Garbo—which was what she was always called in the newspapers and magazines—had developed a reputation for reclusiveness. It was said of her that she refused to see anyone but the friends she chose to see. She was dressed in blue slacks and a white silk blouse, with a patterned silk scarf tied around her head, covering most of her dark hair. Her eyes were hidden behind dark sunglasses. She approached the First Lady readily enough, extending her hand, and saying in her characteristic low, smooth voice that she was honored.

"I am pleased to meet you, Miss Garbo. I have seen you on the screen several times."

"Please, my dear lady," said Garbo. "Call me Greta."

"Well . . . of course, Greta. And I am Eleanor. To you, too, Amelia."

"I am not sure," said Garbo, "that we will ever manage to overcome good manners sufficiently to address the First Lady by her first name."

"If you don't, I shall revert to 'Miss Garbo.' But, tell me, how do you two happen to know each other?"

"We were both admirers of the same man," said Garbo. "Amelia's husband. We met at a strange, grand party Amelia's father hosted in Idaho some years ago. A thing you do in Hollywood: go to big parties when you are invited."

"Ronald Coleman came," said Amelia. "Ethel Barrymore. Cecil B. DeMille. Others . . . all of them celebrities. When daddy invited people, most of them came."

"Whether they wanted to or not," added Garbo.

Amelia laughed. "Whether they wanted to or not. We are having drinks, Eleanor. Will you?"

"Ordinarily I don't, before evening," said Mrs. Roosevelt. "An exception today perhaps. Is that Scotch you are drinking?"

"Single-malt," said Amelia.

"A very small one, please."

Several plates on a wrought-iron table offered light snacks. The First Lady picked up a finger sandwich, bit into it, and was surprised to find that it was smoked salmon with caviar.

"A fine day," she said.

It was in fact a fine day. A few white clouds rode a light breeze across a bright blue sky. The breeze rippled the great meadow behind the house, the way a breeze ripples the smooth water of a lake. Half a mile from the house a woman dressed in white rode a horse at a gallop, away from the house, toward Bull Run. Mrs. Roosevelt thought she rode recklessly and wondered who she was.

"I'd like to show you where we swim," said Amelia. "Bring your glass. It's a short walk."

Mrs. Roosevelt had noticed that a small grove of big oak trees remained in the meadow to the left of the house and halfway between the terrace and Bull Run. It was toward that grove, and not toward Bull Run, where she had supposed they might swim, that Amelia and Garbo now led her.

The grove proved to shelter a grotto: a depression in the meadow, some twelve feet deep, bounded by living stone. The bottom was a round pool, some thirty feet in diameter. Clear water fed into the pool from a spring halfway up the stone wall and ran out through a cleft that formed a tiny brook running toward Bull Run. A redwood picnic bench stood on a ledge to one side of the water. Otherwise the grotto had been left perfectly natural, deep-shaded, private, and so sheltered from the wind that the air below the level of the meadow was actually warmer than that above.

"We did an awful thing," said Amelia. "Put your hand in the water."

Mrs. Roosevelt did. It was warm.

"The spring water is naturally cold," said Amelia. "They used to chill milk and butter in the water. I wanted to swim here, so we hired a contractor to install a heater at the mouth of the spring. You can't see it. We insisted he had to build it so the heater would be invisible. But before the water runs out of the rock and falls into the pool it passes through some tubing that runs over a gas flame."

While Amelia explained this, Garbo quickly stripped off her clothes and plunged into the water. She swam to the far side with strong strokes, then turned and swam back.

"Ahh . . ." she breathed. "It is my favorite place to swim—except only maybe in a roaring surf."

Amelia looked at Mrs. Roosevelt. "Will you join us?" she asked as she lifted her yellow dress over her head.

The First Lady hesitated. It would have been foolish to remark that she had no swimming suit. It would have been more foolish to tell these two young women that never in her life had she swum naked. It would have been more foolish to confess that she had always wanted to.

Here was opportunity. When and where else would she find the privacy? The water was warm. At age fifty-two she was hardly so old she had to deny herself so innocent a pleasure. Undressing was a more complicated undertaking for her than it was for the other two, but in a couple of minutes she finished it and slipped off a rock into the inviting warm water. She tried to swim so as not to get her hair wet, and she paddled about in the grotto, exhilarated and happy she had the mettle to do it.

"How deep is the water?" she asked Amelia.

"The Negroes around here always claimed it is a bottomless hole," said Amelia. "Actually, we had a sash weight on a rope dropped in and found the bottom about thirty feet down. There is a species of fish in the water that a professor from the University of Virginia claims is unique to this water. Little fellows. None more than two inches long. Since we heated the water, they stay down deep mostly, where the water is the temperature they're used to. There are a few turtles in the water. No snapping turtles, I promise you."

"Someone warned me there is a big alligator down deep," said Garbo.

Mrs. Roosevelt laughed. She felt buoyant and essayed a few freestyle strokes, crossing the pool.

They swam for twenty minutes or half an hour, saying little. When Amelia climbed out, the first to do so, Mrs. Roosevelt realized they had no towels. Amelia sat down on one of the benches of the picnic table and stretched. Seeing no alternative, Mrs. Roosevelt sat down a little distance from her and quickly realized the gently stirring warm air of the grotto would dry them after a little time.

Greta Garbo stayed in the water.

"How are you doing, my dear?" the First Lady asked.

"It's hard trying to sort things out," said Amelia. "He had personal ways of arranging things, of keeping records. I've got accountants working on it already, trying to figure out just what he was doing with our money. You know, I gave him control of mine, too. I don't think all his investments were sound. It looks very much like he lost some of my fortune."

"Not enough to—"

"Oh, no. I won't be poor. I'd like to know, though, where some of the money went."

Greta Garbo swam to the edge of the pool nearest them, looked up for a moment; and then, in her distinctive Swedish accent, said, "Mutt and Jeff!"

Mrs. Roosevelt knew exactly what she meant, and laughed. Garbo, who instantly popped playfully beneath the surface, had commented on the two naked figures sitting on the redwood picnic bench: the short, plump Amelia and the tall, thin First Lady. Mutt and Jeff, indeed!

"Damned irreverent Swede!" Amelia laughed.

"She is observant, I'm afraid," said Mrs. Roosevelt.

"Vance swam here with us," said Amelia soberly. "With Garbo and me. Nude. I think he had an affair with her. Briefly."

"The Senator was a popular man," said Mrs. Roosevelt.

Amelia nodded. "So popular somebody murdered him. I wonder if Captain Kennelly is looking for a jealous husband."

During the morning Gerald Baines had identified another person who had left a table in the State Dining room about the same time when Senator Vance Gibson went out.

"I suppose I should have come to you or to the police and made a statement," said Constance Harrison. She received him at the door of her home in Alexandria, Virginia. "Come in, Mr. Baines."

Constance Lewis Harrison was the wife of Judge William A. Harrison of the United States Circuit Court of Appeals. She was a poised and elegant woman of forty years or so, wearing a rose-colored linen jacket and skirt, with a white silk blouse. She wore a single strand of pearls around her neck and a triple strand around her left wrist. Baines knew that her husband, who was twenty-five years older than she, had been a successful corporate lawyer in Richmond before he was appointed to the District Court by Woodrow Wilson in 1918, then to the D.C. Circuit bench by President Roosevelt in 1934. Baines also knew that she was descended from Merriweather Lewis of Lewis and Clark. FFV, she was—First Families of Virginia.

She led Baines into a bright, airy living room furnished in Georgian style. She invited him to sit down and asked if he would like a cup of coffee or tea. He said he would enjoy a cup of coffee, and she rang a little silver bell to summon a black housemaid.

She watched as the maid left the living room, then said, "I am curious as to how you found out about Vance and me."

Baines hoped he concealed his surprise, though he doubted he did. He answered noncommittally, in the hope she would tell something more. "Well," he said, "when someone is murdered, all kinds of people come forward with information that didn't seem important to them when they got it but suddenly seems very important."

Constance Harrison glanced toward the hall leading to the back of the house, probably to be assured that the maid was not where she could overhear the conversation. "His death came as a great shock," she said. "So young and vital, then suddenly— A great shock, particularly when one is compelled to conceal it."

"When he got up and left the State Dining Room, you got up and went, too," said Baines.

"A chance to steal a kiss," she said sadly.

"And did you? I'm sorry, but I need to know if you caught up with him, saw him after he left the dining room."

"Oh, yes. I caught up with him. He said he was feeling nauseous and was on his way to the men's room. We walked along the hall together, and he said he didn't really need to go to the men's room. He said he would just sit down for a while in the East Room. He said it was embarrassing to sit sort of pale and woozy at a table where others were eating, so he'd just sit alone in the East Room for a few minutes, until he recovered. I said I'd stay with him. I was afraid, Mr. Baines, that he might be having a heart attack. But he said, no, if someone came and found us together, we would have to explain. I left him reluctantly. I decided to go to the powder room, so I could walk past the East Room again on my way back to the dining room. That way I could check on him, don't you see?"

Baines nodded. He sensed that the woman was on the verge of tears.

The maid returned carrying a silver coffee service. The coffee obviously had been brewed and was already hot. Mrs. Harrison sat rigid, hardly glancing at the young woman as she put down the tray. She nodded, and the maid left the room again.

Her hands trembled as Mrs. Harrison poured coffee and offered cream and sugar, by gesture, not by words.

"I am sorry to have to put you through such an ordeal," said Baines.

"It's cathartic," she said. "I haven't been able to tell anyone anything about it. I am dismayed that you found out about Vance and me. I thought I had been most circumspect."

"You had been," he said. "I don't think anyone knows."

"Well, obviously someone does."

"The fact that you were absent from the State Dining Room at the time when the Senator was killed is what directed our attention to you," said Baines.

"I see. To continue . . . I did go to the powder room. It was while I was there that I heard Amelia scream."

"Do you know Mrs. Gibson, too?"

"My husband and I have been guests at Fairlea from time to time."

"During the time that—"

"Yes. During that time. I know it sounds callous of Vance and me, Mr. Baines, but I doubt you understand much of the circumstances. Amelia is a boorish woman. Oh, it's true that she brought to the marriage the money that made it possible for the Gibsons to purchase Fairlea and live in great style; but it is also true that the woman was a constant source of embarrassment to Vance. As I suppose you know, she is the daughter of a man who was widely understood to be uncouth, even by whatever standards prevail in Idaho. She herself is only a little short of it—short of uncouth, I mean."

"For example," said Baines.

"Well . . . She swims naked in the lovely little grotto pond behind the house. She encourages others to do the same. One night when we were at the house, Amelia became more than a little tipsy. She decided she wanted to go horseback riding. In the middle of the night. In the dress she had worn at dinner. And she did. She put a bridle on a chestnut mare. No saddle. She climbed on the planks of a stall and threw herself over the mare's back. Astride, of course. She pulled her skirt up around her waist and sat on that horse with her legs and hips exposed, and she trotted off across the meadow toward Bull Run, looking grim and angry. And out there in the dark, we could hear her yelling at someone. And someone yelled back at her: a woman's voice. It sounded like a violent argument. When she came back, she jumped down off her horse right in front of Vance and muttered something like, 'Someday I'm gonna kill that old bitch.' "

Baines shook his head. "It must have been quite a spectacle," he said.

"Vance was deeply humiliated. My husband and I were not the only guests. She displayed her drunkenness and immodesty to six or eight people, including Justice William O. Douglas and Mrs. Douglas. Vance yearned for a different kind of marriage, to a woman with some breeding and polish."

Baines nodded sympathetically. Mrs. Harrison lifted her cup and sipped coffee.

"You could say, I suppose, that a woman hardly shows breeding and polish by having an affair with another woman's husband and in violation of her own marriage vows. But it wasn't just an affair, Mr. Baines. Vance and I were really very deeply in love with each other. We couldn't see how it was all going to come out, but we promised each other we would remain loyal and maybe time would solve the problem for us."

"I have to ask embarrassing questions, Mrs. Harrison. I'm sorry."

"You have to do your job," she said. "Don't apologize."

"Well . . . I suppose you and the Senator had rendezvous. Did you visit him in his apartment?"

"I was never in that apartment. Vance didn't want me to go there. He said it was too public. The neighbors would see. Actually, everywhere is too public when you're having an affair that could create a public scandal. He couldn't come here. I couldn't go to Fairlea. We met at a little country inn on Annandale Road. Afternoons. Usually only once a week, though sometimes twice."

Baines drew a deep breath and let it out slowly, rubbing his fingertips together. "Mrs. Harrison," he said, "in view of what you've told me about your relationship with Senator Gibson and your respect for him, it is difficult for me to raise the question I'm about to ask. But the man was murdered, and I have to ask. Do you think it is possible that the Senator was *not* ill when you saw him in the hall and he went in the East Room?"

"Do you suggest he was lying? Why would he do that?"

"Because he was supposed to *meet* someone in the East Room. Because he had agreed to see someone there. He needed to be alone there, so he asked you not to stay with him. And of course the person he met was the murderer."

"Do you have evidence of that?"

"No. I'm speculating."

"Are you speculating too that I might have killed him?"

"No. If you had, there would have been blood on your clothes, at least on your shoes. Whoever killed him hid the razor in the piano—and smeared blood across the floor between the body and the piano."

She shuddered.

"We are looking for a motive, Mrs. Harrison. Did you ever suspect that Senator Gibson had . . . any other love affairs. I mean recently."

"I'm absolutely sure he didn't. Absolutely certain. He was a very decent man, married to a woman he could no longer love, and he was in love with me."

When Ed Kennelly showed his badge at the receptionist's desk in the symphony office, he was given no illusion that he was welcome. The woman working at that desk somehow managed to slip into their only momentary conversation the fact that she was a volunteer, at the same time conveying by her tone that she regarded a police officer as something that had crawled in off the street and was to be gotten rid of as soon as possible.

She had chosen the wrong man to treat that way. Kennelly told her briskly that he wanted to talk to whoever was in charge of the office and wanted to talk to him right now.

"I am not sure Mr. Tatum is available right now," said the woman.

"I am not sure you quite understand me, ma'am," said Kennelly. "I am Captain Edward Kennelly, District police, homicide squad. I am investigating a murder, and if Mr. Tatum can't make himself available to me here right now, he will have to make himself available to me at headquarters a little later."

The woman flounced out of the room, and in a moment a rail-thin, sepulchral-looking man came out and said in a gravelly voice inflected with a tone of chronic weariness and skepticism that he was Leonard Tatum, general manager of the symphony, and what could he do for Captain Kennelly?

"Sit down with me in your office and talk a minute or two," said Kennelly.

Tatum winced as if he had been handed a traffic ticket and gestured in the direction of his office, down a hall. Kennelly followed him into that office, sat down, and lit a cigarette.

"A homicide investigation," said Tatum. "Whatever could I possibly know about a homicide?"

"You know enough to know that our conversation must be kept absolutely confidential," said Kennelly.

The man nodded. "Yes, I know that."

"All right. According to the Washington *Star,* the symphony received a gift of $500 recently from Miss Joanne Winthrop."

"It was $250."

"Okay, $250. What I need to know is, on what bank did she write the check?"

"That is something I wouldn't know. We keep no records of the banks on which our donors' checks are written. In this one case, however, I can tell you. Miss Winthrop's gift was not by check. She gave us cash."

"How did the *Star* know she gave you money?"

"A donor of $250 was entitled to a sponsor's table. The *Star* exaggerated the amount of the gift, as it exaggerates everything."

*   *   *

"So far as I can tell by a couple more inquiries, she didn't even have a checking account. She paid all her obligations by cash."

"When are you going to question Miss Winthrop, Captain Kennelly?" asked Mrs. Roosevelt.

"Tomorrow, I think. Miss Frelinghuysen insists Miss Winthrop is too ill to see anyone."

"So . . . Well, I met this afternoon with a woman who thinks she was Senator Gibson's one true love," said Baines.

They had met, as was their custom when they were working together on an investigation, in the First Lady's study, where she sipped tea but had offered the men drinks of whisky. She stood for the moment at a window, looking out over the south lawn and the Ellipse, on to the Washington Monument. Everything beyond the Monument was obscured by a drizzle that had begun to fall from low-hanging clouds. At a late-afternoon hour when the sun should still have been shining, automobile headlights gleamed yellow on wet streets, and the lights were on in buildings.

"I met still another who probably had a brief affair with the Senator," said Mrs. Roosevelt.

"This woman is actually pitiable in her innocent assurance that the man loved her and her alone. Unless she is lying or believes a fantasy, he told her he did."

"I'm afraid the Senator was not a very nice man," said Mrs. Roosevelt. "Who is this woman, Mr. Baines?"

"Her name is Constance Harrison. She's the wife of Judge William Harrison of the D.C. Circuit. Our calls about people who left the State Dining Room about the time Senator Gibson did produced her name. She went out when he did in the hope of stealing a moment alone with him, for a kiss."

"I believe I have met Mrs. Harrison," said Mrs. Roosevelt. "A lady of formidable antecedents, I believe."

"And utterly scornful of Mrs. Gibson, both personally and

for *her* antecedents. You should hear her accounts of some of Mrs. Gibson's antics. She invites her friends to swim naked with her in a pond on the estate!"

"Oh, well . . ." said the First Lady. "I suppose we shouldn't condemn her for that."

"She saw the Senator in the hall and in the East Room. She went on to the powder room and was there when she heard Mrs. Gibson scream."

"What can we do in a circumspect way to look into the Gibson family finances?" asked Mrs. Roosevelt. "Amelia suspects her husband had lost a lot of money lately, in bad investments she thinks. She mentioned the name of a firm of accountants who did their tax returns and so forth. I wonder if we can look into any of that?"

"All we need is her consent," said Kennelly.

"What if we don't have it?"

Kennelly shrugged. "Where there's a will there's a way," he said blandly.

"I can't help but wonder, gentlemen, if we are not giving too much attention to the scandals surrounding Senator Gibson's recent life—and too little to the actual murder."

"We are going to have to look into the McGinnis possibility," said Kennelly grimly. "I guess I've been avoiding it."

"Well, then," said Mrs. Roosevelt. "Perhaps tomorrow."

For his cocktail hour that afternoon the President received only one guest. Even Missy was not present as the President sat closeted with Bernard Baruch. As he well knew, Baruch had private and confidential sources of information that came to him from the business community, often from people who would not confide in the President of the United States. Like the Rothschild bankers in London whose private intelligence and communications system brought them the news of the outcome of the Battle of Waterloo hours before the King's ministers received it, Baruch's business contacts in Europe often sent him coded telegrams that told him things Army Intelligence would have liked to know.

Baruch was a tall, erect man with white hair. He had been a boxer in college and still had the square, sturdy physique of an athlete. Like the President, he wore a pince-nez. Unlike the President, he wore his on a black ribbon and could let it drop to his chest when he didn't want it. He pleased the President by sharing the pitcher of martinis that were a Rooseveltian specialty, in which the President took a certain pride.

"The French government has abandoned Paris," said Baruch somberly. "I speak of the government of France. In point of fact, there really is no such thing. Some of the ministers have been out of contact for many hours and may have been captured by the Germans. Premier Reynaud has moved into a château near Tours, with his mistress the Comtesse de Portes. The château has only one telephone line, and it doesn't always work."

"Where is the French line, Bernie?" the President asked. Though most people who knew Baruch well enough to use a nickname called him Barney, the President and Mrs. Roosevelt had always called him Bernie. "Where is the front?"

"There is no front. There is no intact line. The French army is disintegrating. A few units hold in selected places. West of Paris, the line, such as it is, is south of the Seine."

"Paris?"

Baruch shook his head. "The Germans can be there tomorrow if they make a drive for it. My sources say they are coming on methodically and will take two or three more days. Churchill flew over to meet with Reynaud. He's there now."

The President shook his head. "Well, Bernie," he said, "I guess we have to face it. It's hard to think of Paris under German occupation."

The corners of Baruch's mouth turned down. His face was

gradually reddening. "I have to think of French Jews, also of American Jews living in France. I have to wonder what will become of Gertrude Stein, for instance. She's a curious old character, not really my sort of person, but I asked for word of her and have heard nothing."

"There's nothing I can do, Bernie. You know that? There's nothing I can do."

"Except run for another term," said Baruch gravely. "Frank, you've got to do that."

"I have to think about it, anyway."

"You lost a good internationalist in the death of Vance Gibson. The newspapers are being unkind about what they call the lack of progress in the investigation. Has there been no progress?"

"I can't say there has. I don't have time to follow it. You'll have to ask Babs."

"Perhaps I shall. Is she at home?"

"At this time of day, I should imagine so."

The President picked up the telephone and asked the operator to ring the First Lady's study. She was in fact at home, and he asked her to come out and say hello to Bernard Baruch.

After they had exchanged pleasantries, Baruch asked her directly if there had been any progress in the investigation into the murder of Senator Gibson.

"A great deal of information has been discovered," she told him. "I can't see where it leads. I've had a little experience with this sort of thing, you know, and it suggests that the best way of solving a mystery is to accumulate all the information you can—after which you have to try to organize it so that it leads you somewhere."

"Let me guess what you've found out so far," said Baruch with a faint smile. "You've learned that the man was a scandalous philanderer."

"Yes. We've learned that."

"How did he ever manage to keep that a secret for so long?" the President asked.

"He didn't really," said Baruch. "Some people knew."

"He seems to have lost a great deal of money lately," said Mrs. Roosevelt. "I have to wonder if he was a betting man as well. His widow seems to think he lost money on bad investments. Is there a way of tracking that, Bernie? Is there a way of tracking it with some degree of confidentiality?"

"Do you want my help" asked Baruch.

"Could you? Could you look into that aspect of the case for us?"

"Certainly," said Baruch. "I'll be glad to help."

VIII

The President had been looking forward to the evening. On three evenings each year he got away from the White House and went to a stag dinner. Twice a year it was the dinner of the Gridiron Club. Tonight it was the annual dinner of the Capitol Hill Democrats Club, usually known as C.H.D.C.

These dinners were governed by three strict traditions that were never broken. First, that only club members and their guests could be admitted. Second, that no women were allowed. Third, that nothing said at the dinners was to be reported, or even repeated. They were occasions when the President could speak off the record, confident that nothing he said would appear in the newspapers—and this was true even though the Gridiron Club was an organization of journalists.

So few women were members of Congress that hardly anyone ever suggested that the Capitol Hill Democrats Club should admit them to its dinners. Mrs. Roosevelt was among the women not invited.

One reason for the exclusion of women was that the members enjoyed some entertainment that was considered a bit too racy for ladies. The entertainment usually included a few skits, some with bawdy songs, short speeches by Democratic leaders, a speech by the President—when the President was a Democrat—and then usually a few young women dancing in costumes that were abbreviated to begin with and became more abbreviated during their performance.

The dinner was always excellent, especially since Franklin D. Roosevelt became President and it became known that White House meals were worse than bland. Prohibition had never inhibited the free spirits of the C.H.D.C. Dinner would be preceded by cocktails. Fine wines would be served with dinner. Brandy would be offered with the cigars.

The President arrived about eight, wheeled in by Secret Service agents, wearing black tie, cigarette holder atilt. He was ebullient.

Among the members who clustered around the President's wheelchair and enthusiastically welcomed him were Carter Glass and Harry Byrd of Virginia, Champ Clark and Harry Truman of Missouri, Theodore Green of Rhode Island, Walter George of Georgia, Kenneth McKellar of Tennessee, Theodore Bilbo of Mississippi, Cotton Ed Smith of South Carolina, J. William Fullbright of Arkansas, and Tom Connally, Sam Rayburn, and Lyndon Johnson of Texas. All was forgiven for the evening. The President had done all he could to defeat the conservative Senator George in the Georgia Democratic primary in 1938, but the victorious senator shook his hand as warmly as did any other Democrat. Senator Bilbo was an outspoken and dedicated racist, but the President shook his hand, too.

Much of the humor of the evening focused on the question of whether or not the President would run for a third term. Four can-can girls danced and sang—

> In the southern part of France
> The women wear no pants,
> But we bet they know

Whether he will run or no.
So why won't he confide in us?
Why won't he confide in us?
Da-da-da-da-da-da, dum-dum-dum.
Da-da-da-da-da-da, tum-tum-tum.

The can-can dancers did wear pants. Two of the exotic dancers who appeared later did not.

When the President rose to make the principal speech of the evening, he addressed the third-term question—

"The question that seems to attract the greatest interest among some of the newspapers is *not* whether I will stand for election to a *third* term but whether I will run for a . . . *ninth* term."

He was referring to a syndicated column that had suggested a man who would run for a third term could just as readily run for a fourth, fifth, sixth, and so on. The crowd laughed.

"Why . . . at the end of a ninth term, I should be eighty-nine years old! The year would be 1971. No! No, please. It is just *too much.* I assure you— I give you this evening my unqualified assurance. Eight terms is the absolute limit. I will never run for a ninth. I am a firm believer in an eight-term tradition. I would even support a constitutional amendment, limiting any President to eight terms."

They roared.

Word was passed from table to table that in the penthouse of the hotel, later, a pair of girls would give a "wrestling bares" show. The President was invited, but he declined. He left for the White House and his bed by eleven o'clock.

Representative Howard McGinnis was a stocky fifty-year-old man with a fringe of reddish hair around his pink and liver-spotted bald dome. He had a wide mouth with thin white lips and pale blue eyes under thin red eyebrows. Jerry Baines and Ed Kennelly stood at the bar, sipping beer, and trying not to be conspicuous in eyeing him.

For two days a couple of plainclothes sergeants had been tailing McGinnis, making notes of where he went and who he saw. They had not compiled anything on him; the time had been too short to establish any kind of a pattern. This evening they had called in about nine o'clock to say they had tailed McGinnis to a nightclub about halfway between Washington and Baltimore. If anyone wanted to confront him in circumstances away from Capitol Hill and his official office and position, this might be a good place. He had rushed to the bar and seemed to be settling in for the evening.

Baines and Kennelly needed the better part of an hour to reach the nightclub. They did not identify themselves at the door but paid the cover charge of two dollars each and walked to the bar to find a vantage point from which to survey the place.

Called The Clock, the nightclub was archetypal of every suburban roadhouse in the country: a combination cocktail bar, strip joint, and gambling room, all built into a big one-story frame building. A huge clock surrounded by pink neon tubes identified the place to visitors approaching from Washington or Baltimore. Inside, a similar gaudy clock shed a pink light over the stage, the dance floor, and the bar. The gambling room, set a little apart and behind, yet visible from everywhere inside, was lighted by fixtures hanging above the tables. There were a thousand like places across America, ten percent of them at least named The Clock.

The gambling was simple, only two blackjack tables and a craps table, plus a counter at the rear where people were betting on dice that fell through the narrow mouth of an hourglass-shaped wire cage turned by a handle.

Most of the crowd were at the bar or at the tables around the raised platform that constituted a stage and were watching a woman with coarse features, rigidly marcelled blondish hair, and vacant eyes, who looked to be more than forty years old, going awkwardly through the motions of a sinuous dance, to the music of a piano, a saxophone, and drums. She was naked above the waist and was pretending with apathetic gestures that she was about to take off what she wore below: a sequined white G-string and a dozen strings of little white beads that hung to her knees and swung and shimmered as she moved.

The air in the place was heavy with cigarette smoke and with a suggestive atmosphere contrived to insinuate sin and debauchery. The contrivance was at variance with reality. The stripping and gambling were unimaginative. The hookers working the bar were unappealing.

The Clock was not unappealing to some prominent men, though. Looking around the room, Baines immediately spied Representative Martin Dies of Texas, the notorious bullying chairman of the House Committee on Un-American Activities. Wilbur Mills, the first-term Representative from the Second District of Arkansas, sat with Representative Howard McGinnis.

The stripper did not take off her G-string, and when she strode off the stage the announcer came on the overamplified public address system and pleaded, "C'mon, folks! A big hand for Sister Aimee! A *big* hand! You're gonna tell your grandkids you saw Sister Aimee at The Clock!"

It seemed odd to Baines and Kennelly, but the crowd did applaud then. The woman, who had covered herself with a silk shawl, came out and bowed awkwardly, opened the shawl and exposed her breasts, then hurried offstage.

"Who the hell is she?" Kennelly asked the man beside him at the bar. "We came in after she was already on stage."

The man swung around on his stool, and Kennelly realized he was Congressman Dirksen from Illinois. "You didn't recognize her?" he asked in his deep, mellifluous voice. "That lady, sir, is Aimee Semple McPherson, or what's left of her. When people lost interest in her Four Square Gospel and when she couldn't keep the tabernacle open anymore, she tried tent revivals. But that didn't draw either, or hasn't for the last five or six years. So, she's reduced to removing her clothing in public to earn her bread."

"I'd say she's doing what she always did best," said Kennelly dryly. "Making a spectacle of herself."

Congressman Dirksen smiled, but he said, "She's a servant of God."

Baines watched McGinnis, who was engaged in animated conversation with Wilbur Mills. The animated nature of the conversation apparently came from the bottle that sat on the table between them, from which each man poured shots. They laughed heartily, so much that they attracted attention even from a crowd that was raucous itself.

"Captain Kennelly. We seem to run into each other everywhere."

He turned and found himself facing Lena Madison. She was wearing the uniform worn by waitresses at The Clock: a simple white blouse and a hip-high black skirt.

"Lena," he said. "What are you doing here?"

"I work here," she said. "I have to make a living, 'specially since I just lost one good job."

Kennelly nodded at Baines. "Meet Jerry Baines of the Secret Service. Jerry, this is Lena Madison."

"You're as attractive as Ed told me you were," said Baines gallantly.

"It's no coincidence, Lena, that you were working in Senator Gibson's apartment and also for Misses Frelinghuysen and Winthrop. It's also obvious that you weren't telling me the entire truth last Friday."

"No, sir, I wasn't."

"You knew who Miss Tareytons was."

"Yes, sir. And you know too, now—I guess."

"Yes. I do. Want to amend your story?"

She glanced around the room. "They aren't going to allow

me to stand here and talk to you. I can sit down at a table with you. Then you have to buy me a 'drink.' You know what I mean."

"The Secret Service has a good expense account," said Baines as he slipped off his bar stool.

"I want a table close to that one," said Kennelly, nodding toward the table where McGinnis sat with Mills.

Lena led them to a table to the right of that one. Kennelly made a point of sitting with his back to the two congressmen, on the chair closest to them.

"Tell me how the 'coincidence' happened," said Kennelly to Lena.

"I've worked for Miss Frelinghuysen for about two years. I was working for her when Miss Winthrop moved in with her. That was about Thanksgiving time, last year. Sometime after Christmas Miss Frelinghuysen called me in, told me to sit down, and she told me the story. Miss Winthrop was seeing Senator Gibson, and the senator wanted her to spend some nights with him in his apartment. But his wife might come to that apartment, and she must never see any evidence that another woman had been there. So if I wanted the job, I could come and clean the place early every morning—and get paid good for it, too—and still be able to get to my other people's homes on time. It was a good deal. I took the job. Pretty soon I began to see the same cigarette butts in the apartment ashtrays as I saw in Miss Frelinghuysen's ashtrays. Herbert Tareyton cigarettes."

"Who's Miss Kools, then?"

"I never did figure that one out. At first I supposed the Kools butts were Mrs. Gibson's. Then one morning at Miss Frelinghuysen's place I saw a newspaper story one of them had left on the coffee table. There was a picture of Mrs. Gibson at some kind of charity affair in Alexandria. The story said she'd had a supper at her home after the affair. So I knew she didn't spend the night in the Senator's apartment, and the Kools butts I'd dumped that morning weren't hers."

Kennelly grinned and spoke to Baines. "I told you she'd make a good detective. I wish I could hire you, Lena."

"Ain' no nigguh nevah gone be no D.C. *po*-lice detective," she said, mimicking an accent she had obviously been at pains to eliminate. "Same as none ain' nevah gone come in *dis* place, 'cept as a servant. Not even as a hooker. I's 'lowed to cadge drinks, gent'mens. I's 'lowed to let you feel me up heah at this table. I ain' 'lowed to take a gent'man to none o' the rooms out back."

"I am glad of the latter," said Baines.

A waiter appeared with a small glass of what proved to be iced tea, for Lena, and two bottles from which the two men could take their choice of rye or Scotch. He handed them a bill and asked them to pay in advance. The iced tea cost $2.50, a bottle $15.00.

"You can take what you don't drink home," said Lena. "Souvenir of the evening: the most expensive bottle of Scotch you ever bought." She shrugged. "And you can feel me up all you want."

Baines paid.

"You told me you saw the Kools first, then they tapered off until you saw nothing but Tareytons. Do you want to make any change in that?"

"No, sir."

"Anything else in the story that you want to change?"

"No. I just supposed that if Miss Frelinghuysen or Miss Winthrop suspected I'd told you that Miss Winthrop was Miss Tareytons, I'd lose another job. And I didn't know you well enough to know if I could trust you not to tell them."

"I understand," said Kennelly. "If you're not going to wind up living in the alleys, you've got to work at every job you can get."

"Captain Kennelly . . . my family lives on The Hill. You know where I mean? Georgia Avenue. My brother is going to be a *dentist!* Every member of the family has got to support himself . . . herself. Or go where you said, to live in the alleys, where six, eight families get cold water from one outdoor spigot, maybe use the same privy. I—"

"Understood, Lena," said Kennelly. "I figured it out the morning when I met you. So anything you say is confidential. Jerry and I tell nothing to the Misses Frelinghuysen and Winthrop."

"They're good girls, basically," said Lena. "Just never had to live in the real world."

"Change the subject," said Baines. "Do you know the two congressmen at the next table?"

She nodded. "Congressman from Ohio and congressman from somewhere down South."

"Do they come here often?"

"The one from Ohio does. The one from down South, just now and then. He's come more often since Sister Aimee came to work. The one that was sitting by you at the bar—Mr. Dirksen from Illinois—he's got a crush on Sister Aimee, keeps trying to date her. He keeps telling this lunatic story to anybody who'll listen, about how God saved him from a heart attack; and he seems to think she had something to do with it, by praying for him or something."

"She's really Aimee Semple McPherson?" Kennelly asked.

Lena nodded. "So they say. Came on bad times after faking that kidnapping. She went too far that time. Lo, how the mighty have fallen! She takes pills and drinks, they say. You know what that combination is going to do to her."

"The one from Ohio is called McGinnis," said Kennelly. "You say he's here often?"

"Two nights a week, average. I can tell you something else about him. He never pays a check. Never."

"Who pays?"

"I don't know. He's 'connected.' You know what that word means?"

"Connected to the gangs," said Kennelly.

She shrugged. "Who else doesn't pay his check?"

"His connection is supposed to be to the insurance industry," said Baines. "Not to organized crime."

Lena shrugged again. "Tell me the distinction."

"His connection to the insurance industry would give him a reason to want to see Senator Gibson dead," said Kennelly.

"Who do we know whose money comes one hundred percent from the insurance business?" she asked.

"Who do you have in mind?"

"Miss Winthrop," said Lena. "Miss Frelinghuysen. Two family fortunes, Miss Winthrop's from her father's big agency in Boston, Miss Frelinghuysen's from her family's big stockholding interest in Northeast Fire and Casualty. Servants notice the mail they throw out in the trash."

Kennelly grinned. "I bet you can do better than that," he said. "Holding envelopes up to the light—How much does Joanne Winthrop get from her family?"

"One hundred dollars a month," said Lena. "About what I make from all my jobs."

"She doesn't live on that," said Baines. "She—"

"She had to get money from somewhere else," said Lena. "Miss Frelinghuysen's checks come to more than five hundred a month."

"Remind me," said Kennelly to Baines. "If I ever get rich enough to hire somebody to work in my house, to get a post office box and have all my mail delivered there."

"Don't be careless, anyway," said Lena. "Don't assume your nigger household servants are deaf, dumb, and blind."

"Does McGinnis meet people here?" Kennelly asked.

"Sure. It's early. Nurse that bottle, and you'll see some guys."

Not very often did the First Lady have the privilege of spending an evening without an obligation, without an appointment. This evening she had the privilege, and she ate her dinner from a tray brought up from the kitchen. She was not alone. Her long-time friend Lorena Hickock had moved into the White House and was occupying the third-floor rooms that had been Louis Howe's. Hick—as she was called—had a tray, too. The two women ate and listened to a shortwave radio Mrs. Roosevelt had had installed in her bedroom. The past few weeks she had listened as often as she could. She understood French, and the news from France, where it was now early morning, was deeply distressing.

Hick picked without enthusiasm at the serving of tuna casserole that was their dinner. White House food was so bad that she went out for most of her meals, sometimes even having them delivered. It was the one thing with which she could not be in sympathy with the First Lady. The President made bitter jokes about the ill-prepared, tasteless food from White House kitchen. Eleanor seemed oblivious either to his jokes or the food itself.

The two women were wearing nightgowns. Mrs. Roosevelt sat propped against the headboard. Hick sat at the foot of the bed. Putting her tray aside, she began to massage the First Lady's feet.

"You are a darling," said Mrs. Roosevelt softly.

"If it makes you more comfortable . . . I would do anything to make you more comfortable. You seem so tired."

"I am frightened, Hick . . ."

Lorena Hickock was a big, solid woman, almost as tall as the First Lady and heavier by twenty pounds or more. She had been a newspaper reporter, assigned to cover Mrs. Roosevelt in the campaign of 1932. They had become close friends. Hick became a confidante, indeed the only person in whom Mrs. Roosevelt fully confided her feelings about many things. When they were apart, she wrote long letters to Hick—and received long letters in return. To be closer, Hick gave up journalism and took a job with the government.

Now she lived in the White House. Even so, they did not see each other daily. The demands on the First Lady denied her the time she would have liked to devote to her friend.

"What are you afraid of, Eleanor?" Hick asked.

"War," sighed Mrs. Roosevelt. "War and death. I can't expect to live through a war and lose . . . Hick! Many mothers will lose their sons! I have four. And a husband who—Hick, I am bound to lose at least one of them!"

The First Lady sobbed and covered her face with her hands.

Lorena Hickock leaned forward over her and clasped Mrs. Roosevelt's legs. She kissed her knees, through her nightgown. "I will always be here to comfort you," she whispered.

"Oh, I know you will, Hick. I know you will!"

Lena Madison had drunk two more glasses of iced tea, and the bill for iced tea had now come to $7.50. She told Baines that $2.50 of that was hers, and she would repay him.

He shrugged. "In a federal budget of *billions* of dollars," he said, "I guess we can pay for some consulting detective work."

Howard McGinnis and Wilbur Mills remained at the table next to theirs. Three more women had come out to dance on the little stage, and now "Sister Aimee" came out for her second appearance of the evening. Neither Baines nor Kennelly had ever seen her in person before, but the tragic, yet defiant, set of her jaw suggested strongly that she was in fact the faded evangelist of the Four Square Gospel who had ruined her reputation by faking her own kidnapping in 1926 and had been in spiraling decline ever since. Her vacuous eyes were unmistakably those of a dedicated evangelist. Apparently "Sister Aimee" really was Sister Aimee.

It was impossible not to stare at the stripper, knowing who she was. But when she was about halfway through her performance, Lena nudged Kennelly's arm and tossed her chin toward the table where the two congressmen sat.

Kennelly glanced. A young woman was sitting down with McGinnis and Mills. She, too, was staring at the stage and did not notice Kennelly's glance.

"I am going to keep my back toward that table," muttered Kennelly. "Don't stare at them. Jerry . . . The girl who's just joined Howard McGinnis is Laura Mason."

Baines turned and took a good look.

"What are they doing?" Kennelly asked.

"I can't tell. There doesn't seem to be any love lost between them. Unless I misunderstand what I just saw, she's turned down the offer of a drink."

"Which one is she talking to?"

"Let me tell you," said Lena. "I'm the one facing them, and I'm obviously just a short-skirted nigger."

"Lena—" murmured Kennelly with a deep frown, meaning to tell her not to disparage herself that way.

"She's talking hard and fast to McGinnis. Mills is watching Sister Aimee and paying them no attention."

Kennelly pretended to be staring at the dancer, who had just won a round of applause by baring her breasts.

"Buying and selling," said Lena quietly. "She just gave him something, and he just gave her something I'd guess is money."

Baines turned and looked. "Now they're looking glum, like neither one of them is happy with the transaction. I wish I could hear what they're saying."

"She's not staying," said Lena. "She's getting up and leaving."

"If we were in the District, I'd stop McGinnis and see what he bought, even if I didn't have a warrant," said Kennelly.

"Don't forget he's a congressman," said Baines.

"Well, by God, *she* isn't," said Kennelly. "I can nab her.

We square on the check here? Let's go! Thanks, Lena. We'll see if we can't do something for you."

Outside, they saw that Laura Mason had come to The Clock in a taxi.

"That's not cheap," said Kennelly. "Our poor little government girl and would-be lawyer spent some bucks to get out here and back tonight."

"They're getting away."

"No, they're not. I'm not going to stop them until they're back inside the District. Might as well wait till I've got jurisdiction."

The cab driver took Highway 1 for his route back to Washington. Kennelly kept close behind him as they drove through College Park, along the edge of the campus of the University of Maryland. In Hyattsville the highway became Rhode Island Avenue. As they crossed the District line, Kennelly used his radio to alert any police car on Rhode Island that he was following a suspect and expected to make a stop. Twelfth Precinct responded that it could put a car on the avenue to assist in the stop. Shortly the patrol car came up behind. Kennelly signaled him to stop the taxi, and the patrolmen switched on their red flashers and pulled the taxi over to the curb.

Kennelly walked up to the car. He opened the back door and shook his head at Laura Mason. "Naughty, naughty," he said. "I'm afraid you're going to have to come with me."

"Why?" the red-haired young woman protested. "What for?"

"Your little transaction," said Kennelly. "Right under the eyes of the cops. We were watching him and were surprised to see you. C'mon, now. We're going in to headquarters."

"Hey!" yelled the cab driver. "Who pays me?"

"Wanta pay the man? You collected the money."

*   *   *

"I'm doing you a big favor, Miss Mason," said Kennelly. They had stopped short of police headquarters, at an all-night diner, and were sitting in a booth with three mugs of steaming coffee on the table before them. "The coffee at headquarters is so bad I sometimes wonder how they managed to make it."

"Not as bad as the tuna-salad sandwiches at the White House," said Baines.

"Anyway," said Kennelly to Laura Mason, "I figured maybe we could talk a while here, and maybe it won't be necessary for you to go to headquarters at all. If I take you in there this time of night, it'll be tough to keep reporters from seeing you. What's more, I sure don't wanta lock you up. So don't make it necessary for me."

The young woman nodded glumly. Her voice had broken as she talked with them in the car. She was conspicuously miserable: face flushed, jaw trembling.

"Now. My back was to you. If I'd turned around and you'd seen me, you wouldn't have done what Agent Baines and another witness saw you do. Yesterday you told me you thought Congressman McGinnis murdered Senator Gibson. Tonight you met him at The Clock and handed him something, in return for which he handed you what was obviously money."

She lit a cigarette. "You want to know what I sold him," she said.

"I want to know what you sold him."

"I sold him two letters from Senator Gibson's files."

"Specifically?"

"I told you that Senator Gibson was collecting dirt on Howard McGinnis. I told you why. McGinnis was collecting dirt on him, too, and he had some. Nothing as bad as what I sold him tonight."

"What did these letters say?"

"I can show you. I wasn't fool enough to sell him the only copies. I had photostats made."

"Maybe we ought to look at these photostats. Even yet tonight."

In her apartment on West Virginia Avenue, Laura Mason laid the letters in front of Kennelly and Baines.

The first was a handwritten letter—

July 3, 1935

Dear Russ,

If you read this letter, I will be dead. I will be if you trusted me and did what I told you, which was not to open the envelope except if I was dead. You should now hand this letter to the police, because if I am dead it will be for sure that I have been murdered.

You will have got it figured out, I imagine, but this letter is the evidence that will tell you for sure that Howard killed me to keep my mouth shut. I have spent nights the better part of the last six months checking the books of the agency. In the morning I am going to face Howard with what is absolutely true—that he has been knocking down for many years and has cheated me out of many thousands of dollars. Before I tell him what I know, I will tell him I have placed this letter in your hands and in the hands of several others. (Actually, it's only in your hands, but he won't know that.) I am not afraid of him. I will have a gun in my pocket when I face him. But who knows what will happen? Whatever, it's the Lord's will.

I'd almost rather lose the money than go through what I'm going to go through in the morning. But Howard is a thoroughly bad man, and if he gets away with it again he will just go on doing it, till there's nothing left at all. Be careful how you handle this. He's got lots of political influence as you know. I'm not sure who you should go to, maybe to the F.B.I. Be careful.

Your brother,
Bun

The second letter was typed—

Dear Senator Gibson,

I have been told on good authority that you are looking into the doings of Representative Howard McGinnis. I write to you and am enclosing a letter I received on the day of the death of my dear brother Bernard. He was partner for many years to Congressman McGinnis, and I think for the rest his letter explains itself.

I am ashamed to say that I never showed my brother's letter to anyone. My reasons were that I had to believe that nobody in this State would do anything about it. Howard McGinnis is a powerful man, politically. Anyway, how could I prove what my brother said? My brother died in a fire in the insurance agency office. The fire that killed him destroyed all the files and records of the business. Thinking about it over the years since, I have come to the conclusion that the bank records and insurance company records could prove what my brother said. Actually, only the bank records would serve, because the insurance companies their agency represented would never cooperate in an investigation looking for evidence of embezzlement and murder by Howard McGinnis.

Also, I had to face the fact that the political people and insurance companies could impoverish me if I spoke up—not to mention that I might die as my brother did.

As a United States Senator, you may be able to do justice where I never dared to try. I beg you to keep this matter confidential if you can't <u>destroy</u> that evil man.

May the Lord bless you in this work.

Sincerely,
Russell Mayo

"What did he pay you?" Kennelly asked sternly.

"Two hundred dollars," she said. "That's all I asked for. That's all I need to live on through the bar exam."

"Besides," said Kennelly sarcastically, "you were afraid of what he'd do if you asked for more."

Laura Mason nodded soberly.

"Well, sleep tight, Miss Mason. I could send you to sleep in a jail cell. But what the hell . . . I'll expect you to tell the truth if you're asked."

IX

"Mr. President, the murder of Senator Vance Gibson, in the East Room here in the White House, occurred a week ago today. Can you report any progress identifying the murderer?"

"I can't *report* any progress. That is not the same as saying there has been none."

The President lifted his chin, took a puff from his cigarette, and grinned. This was one of the things he did best and enjoyed most: bantering with the press.

"We understand, Mr. President, that the First Lady is participating in the investigation."

"Yes. So am I. So are you. So is everybody who has any ideas to contribute or wishes to encourage those in charge of the investigation."

"But is the First Lady *active* in the investigation?"

"You know my wife. She is active at anything that catches her fancy or inspires her interest."

Presidential press conferences were held in the Oval Office. The reporters gathered around the President's desk. A privileged senior few could sit down. The rest stood. All had their notebooks and pencils at the ready. All scribbled furi-

ously as the President spoke. He spoke always "for attribu-
tion"—meaning that his remarks could be recapitulated by
the reporters from their notes, but he was never to be
quoted directly. If he wanted to be quoted, he handed out
a press release. *That* could be quoted. No one complained of
these rules. He was the most accessible President any of
them could remember. In fact, he was the most accessible
President the United States had ever had.

"Have you any estimate as to when the Gibson murder
case may be solved?"

"Have you any estimate as to when you or I or any of us
will understand Einstein's theory of relativity?"

"What is your best estimate, Mr. President, as to when
the Germans will enter Paris?"

"I am assured by the French Premier, Monsieur Reynaud,
that the French will fight to the bitter end. I need hardly
remind you that the Germans were within forty miles of
Paris in 1914 and again in 1917—and they didn't get there.
The outlook is grim, to be sure. But it has been grim before.
I am confident the gallant French nation will fight on even
if Paris is lost."

"Mr. President, Colonel Charles Lindbergh says the German air force, the *Luftwaffe*, is invincible and will defeat
Great Britain as well as France. Would you care to comment
on that?"

"Colonel Lindbergh surprised me in 1927. He surprises
me now. Colonel Lindbergh is no end of surprises."

"We cannot of course accuse Representative McGinnis of
committing a five-year-old murder," said Mrs. Roosevelt.
"Even if the evidence of these letters were enough to sustain the charge, it bears no relationship to the murder of
Senator Gibson."

"I beg your pardon, ma'am," said Ed Kennelly. "I believe

it does. It's possible that McGinnis knew the Senator had these letters in his files. If he knew—"

"But he would not get them out of there by murdering the Senator," she said.

"No. I suppose not. But it would give him reason for hating the Senator."

"Actually," said Baines, "McGinnis would have had no reason to suppose the Senator's death would be followed by a page-by-page examination of everything in his files. The files, including the Mayo letters, might well have been boxed up and shipped to Idaho, where those letters could have disappeared forever."

"And very likely would have, but for Miss Mason," said Mrs. Roosevelt.

"She's lucky McGinnis didn't kill her," said Kennelly.

"Does either of you think there is any possibility that Miss Mason *forged* those letters?" asked the First Lady. "She has demonstrated a singular want of character. Instead of turning the letters over to some law-enforcement agency, she sold them to Congressman McGinnis. If she's capable of doing that— Well, in any event, I don't see how we can place much confidence in her word."

"Or in his," said Baines. "He bought them."

"Once again," said Mrs. Roosevelt, "we are distracted from the events of last Wednesday evening. Miss Mason wants us to believe Congressman McGinnis murdered Senator Gibson. If he did, how did he get into the White House that evening?"

"Our agents have continued to inquire about people who left the State Dining Room about the time when the Senator left," said Baines. "We haven't come up with any more."

"I believe you've named Congressman Carl Vinson from Georgia, who said he saw no one in the men's room, also Mrs. Everett Dirksen, wife of the Congressman from Illinois, who— Wait a moment! She said she saw no one, either upstairs or downstairs. But Mrs. Harrison said she was in the powder room when she heard Mrs. Gibson scream. How could she have gone down there without encountering Mrs. Dirksen, either in the powder room or on the stairs or in the halls?"

"Not impossible, I suppose," said Baines.

"Well . . . Maybe this is fanciful, but let's imagine a scenario," said Mrs. Roosevelt. "Mrs. Harrison is in love with Senator Gibson. Their affair has been going on for some time, with promises. Suddenly she learns he is seeing another woman, maybe more than one. Hell hath no fury et cetera. She begs him to leave the State Dining Room sometime during dinner, so they can be alone together for a moment, maybe in the East Room. He agrees. They fix an approximate time, say nine o'clock. She leaves her table, goes downstairs, and opens a window to let the murderer into the White House."

"You used just the right word," said Kennelly. "And a favorite of yours. 'Fanciful.' "

"But she has to be lying about going to the powder room. If she had, she'd have seen Mrs. Dirksen. On the other hand . . . Who would she have hired to kill the Senator? Who *could* she have hired? With whom could she have formed an alliance? It is difficult to think she conspired with the likes of Congressman McGinnis."

"I would like the answer to one question," said Baines. "Did she leave her table after the Senator left his, as she says she did—or did she leave earlier?"

Kennelly shook his head. "We're on the wrong track again," he said. "Let's face up to it. In the first place, a *man* killed Senator Gibson. A woman couldn't get a razor to his throat. He'd have struggled. He—"

"A woman he trusted," said Mrs. Roosevelt. "She stood behind him and put her arms lovingly around him, and—"

"Then *why?*" asked Kennelly. "What was the motive? Constance Harrison, the betrayed lover?"

"She could have embraced him from behind," said Mrs.

Roosevelt. "And she was in the White House that evening."

"Joanne Winthrop and Laura Mason, two more betrayed lovers," said Kennelly. "Or . . . for that matter, Amelia Gibson, the betrayed wife. Then we come to the insurance gang. Howard McGinnis. Some thug hired by the insurance boys . . . Or—"

The ringing of Mrs. Roosevelt's telephone interrupted him.

She picked it up and listened. After a moment she put it down and said, "The call was for you, really, Captain Kennelly. It seems there has been a fire. Miss Mason's apartment—"

Kennelly and Baines reached the small square brick apartment building on West Virginia Avenue while the flames still poured from the windows and a stream of burning wood and fabric still rose in a fiery column of white smoke. The unmuffled engines of the fire equipment roared. Streams of water poured into the building from a dozen hoses. The firemen seemed oddly lethargic. They just stood at their hoses, aiming in water they seemed to know would have no effect on the defiant smoky fire.

Both men wore their badges on their jackets as they sought out the commander of the fire battalion.

"Four apartments," the man said. "People home in one, the rest gone. Nobody hurt, so far as we can be sure."

"Arson?" asked Kennelly.

"Funny question," said the white-helmeted fireman. "You got reason to think so?"

"Just an idea," said Kennelly.

"Well, it's possible," said the fireman. "The fire spread awful fast. Like there was an accelerant."

"Where are the people who lived in there?"

"The mother and kids that were home have gone to the woman's sister's place. Girl who lived in one of the apartments is sitting in Pumper 3 over there. She came home as soon as somebody called her. *She* calls it arson."

Laura Mason sat in the seat beside the driver's seat in one of the roaring pumpers. The sympathetic firemen had given her a mug of coffee.

"They knew I wasn't at home," she said numbly to Kennelly and Baines. "They *knew* I wasn't. They burned up my law books and all my notes that I needed to study for the bar examination. My clothes. Everything. Hey . . . Even the two hundred bucks I got from McGinnis last night."

"Why, you figure?" asked Kennelly.

She shrugged. "Not to kill me. They had to know I wasn't home. A warning . . . No. My guess is that whoever did it figured I'd kept copies of what I sold McGinnis last night. Maybe they figured there was more stuff, too. My guess is they burned me out to burn any more papers I had from the Senator's files. Joke's on them. I sold them all I had, last night."

"Joke's on them in a bigger way," said Kennelly. "The copies of the Mayo letters are in my file at headquarters."

Representative Howard McGinnis handed the photostat of the handwritten Bun Mayo letter back to Ed Kennelly, and he smiled wryly and shook his head. "It's like a chain letter, Captain. This must be the sixth or seventh copy I've seen. Where'd you get it?"

"It survived the fire," said Kennelly.

"Survived what fire?"

"Well . . . never mind that. Have you burned the original?"

McGinnis's face hardened. "I think you had better be specific, Captain Kennelly. Just what do you have in mind?"

"You bought the original last night, Congressman," said Kennelly. "At The Clock. In the presence of Representative Mills, who probably didn't know what you were doing but is a witness to the transaction anyway, and under the eyes of two other witnesses. I was the guy with his back to you, at the next table. It was while Sister Aimee was stripping."

McGinnis swelled with indrawn breath. "The little bitch set me up."

"No. She didn't know we were watching. We arrested her last night, not you."

"She's not in custody. She's—"

"Free on her own recognizance, as they say," said Kennelly.

McGinnis leaned back in his chair and lit a cigarette, using the moment to take careful measure of this police captain who had come to his office. "Like I said, Captain, this old thing keeps coming back like a damned chain letter. Mayo took the whole damned thing to the prosecuting attorney in Columbus in 1935. He accused me of murdering his brother. He didn't have a grain of evidence, and the prosecutor couldn't act."

"He wrote to Senator Gibson that he never dared show his brother's letter to anyone."

"Of course he did. Would he send a letter to a senator, asking him to make political hay out of something local authorities already looked into, years before? Hardly. Be realistic about this, Captain. What have you got in mind, anyway? You're investigating the murder, I suppose. You'll have a hell of a time laying that on me. I was at The Clock that night, too, and I can name congressmen who were with me. And, yes, I did buy the letter from Gibson's poor little girl. She offered it, and I bought it. You wanta call it blackmail? Hey! Two hundred goddamned dollars! So the kid can get through her bar examination. That's blackmail?"

"Well, I'm glad we've had this conversation, Congressman."

"I'm glad too, Captain. This old Mayo thing comes up— Well . . . I've said like a chain letter too often. In our Kiwanis Club in Columbus we have a joke necktie. It has to be the ugliest necktie you ever saw. Somebody put it in the Christmas gift exchange one year. Whoever got it wore it once and put it back in the exchange the next year. Captain, you give that tie away, and sooner or later it comes back to you. That's the way it is with the Mayo business. My partner was a silly man. His brother is an ugly man, ugly of mind and spirit, I mean. His accusation keeps coming back to me. You can't take it too seriously. I don't. Not anymore."

"I appreciate your time, Senator Truman," said Baines. "I'll take as little of it as possible."

"At this time of day, my time is available," said Senator Harry Truman. "Would you care for a drink? I usually have one about this time, before I go home to my wife and my daughter."

"I'd appreciate that, Senator," said Baines.

Senator Truman was the archetype of a midwestern farmer: face as open as the prairie, capable of hiding nothing—if he had been interested in hiding anything. That face had been inexpertly scraped with a razor that morning, and his hair had been cut in a style Washington called "white sidewall"—that is, clipper run to the top of the ears. He wore little round gold-framed eyeglasses.

As the Senator from Missouri poured two medium-size shots of bourbon into two glasses, Baines reflected on what he'd heard said of Mr. Truman: that he hadn't the chance of a snowball in hell of being reelected.

As though Senator Truman had read Baines's thought, he said, "Lucky you caught me today. I'm going home tomorrow. Gotta launch my reelection campaign." He handed Baines a glass. "Anyway, what can I do for you, Mr. Baines?"

"At the dinner last Wednesday night—the one when Senator Gibson left his table and was killed—you and Mrs.

Truman were sitting at a table with Judge and Mrs. Harrison. Isn't that right?"

"That's right."

"Did you happen to notice Senator Gibson getting up and leaving?"

"Yes. I thought it was a funny time to be going out."

"Well . . . Can you tell me if Mrs. Harrison left the table and went out *before* Senator Gibson left the table, or *after?*"

The Senator stared into his glass for a moment. "Is that an important question?" he asked.

"The answer could be very important," said Baines.

"Well, let me think. If it's important, I don't want to say wrong. I noticed Vance get up. He and I came here the same year, you know. Fellow Democrats. I got to know him pretty well. Well, let's see. He got up and went out. And then— Then *she* got up and went out. She went out after he did."

"Are you sure of that, Senator?"

Senator Truman grinned. "No. But that's my best impression."

"Can you say if she noticed Senator Gibson getting up and going out?"

"I couldn't say she noticed or didn't. I remember thinking it was a funny time to be leaving the room, because speeches were going to start pretty soon. I thought it was especially funny of Mrs. Harrison."

"Why is that, Senator?"

"Well . . . I hope this isn't indelicate, but I remember thinking the woman must have a pretty small bladder. She'd been out not more than fifteen minutes before."

Brenda Frelinghuysen opened the door, and Ed Kennelly walked again into the apartment she shared with Joanne Winthrop. This time Miss Winthrop was sitting in the living room. Miss Frelinghuysen left the room so Kennelly could talk with Joanne Winthrop alone.

"I knew I'd have to confront the police sooner or later," she said glumly.

The young woman was even more beautiful than her photograph suggested. Her bored expression in the picture he had studied suggested a spoiled young society playgirl. In person she was nothing of the sort. She was poised and so much in command of her presence that it was difficult to imagine that she could have attempted suicide. Her beauty was delicate but not fragile. As Miss Frelinghuysen had received him in white silk hostess pajamas, so did this striking young woman—except only that hers were burgundy. She reached toward an ashtray and crushed her half-smoked cigarette—a Tareyton of course—and faced Kennelly with an expression of concentrated patience.

"I do have to ask a few questions," he said.

She smiled wanly. "You found my fingerprints all over Vance's apartment."

"Yes, we did. But that made little difference. Your fingerprints are not on file, Miss Winthrop. Or weren't until they were taken at the hospital."

"I wasn't aware my fingerprints were taken."

"But they were, probably while you were unconscious. You attempted suicide, Miss Winthrop. You now have a police record."

She looked away from him. "A criminal record. How perfectly lovely."

"Not a criminal record. A medical record. In case you are ever found and must be identified. Not the kind of record that is made available to prospective employers and so on."

"Just the same," she said, "it makes me public property. Somewhere there's a *card* in a *file*, with my name on it and my fingerprints. Did they take my picture, too?"

"Miss Winthrop," said Kennelly. "Suppose I told you I could lift your card from the file. Suppose I told you somebody one hundred percent sympathetic would like to talk to you. How good is your word, Miss Winthrop? Can you keep a confidence?"

Even Joanne Winthrop's poise ebbed when she found herself in the White House—and not only in the White House but in the private quarters of the White House, in the presence of President Roosevelt himself and of his formidable First Lady.

Having received Kennelly's telephone call, Mrs. Roosevelt had made a special request of the President: that he invite no one from outside the intimate circle to his cocktail hour this evening, that she might bring Joanne Winthrop to the West Sitting Room.

No one was there but the President and Mrs. Roosevelt, Missy, Kennelly, and Baines.

"Officially," said Mrs. Roosevelt, "you are not in mourning, not for a man whom *officially* you didn't know. All of us here understand the circumstances, and all of us are sympathetic."

Joanne Winthrop's poise had not disappeared entirely. "I am embarrassed to admit I am a Republican," she said.

The President laughed. "So was my wife's uncle," he said. "Confidentially. I understand there are a few left."

Joanne Winthrop had changed into a dark gray skirt, a white silk blouse, and a hound's-tooth-check jacket for her visit to the White House. She wore a simple necklace of gold set with emeralds and pearls. She sat with her legs crossed at the ankles, and she had pleased the President by accepting and obviously appreciating one of his F.D.R. martinis.

"Miss Frelinghuysen suggests you may be going home to Boston," said Mrs. Roosevelt.

"I believe I shall," said Joanne Winthrop solemnly.

"Miss Winthrop—"

"Please," she interrupted. "Call me Joanne."

The President grinned. "Then we shall all be on the first-name basis."

Joanne Winthrop smiled shyly. "I could never call you or Mrs. Roosevelt by your first names, Mr. President," she said. "But I will feel more comfortable if you call me Joanne."

"Well . . ." said Mrs. Roosevelt tentatively. "We— We know about the relationship between you and Senator Gibson."

"I doubt you know very much about it, to be altogether frank," said Joanne calmly.

"Miss Frelinghuysen told us you are definitely not the kind of girl who enters into casual relationships," said Kennelly. "Nothing out of our investigation says anything contrary."

"I am grateful to Brenda."

"Let us set the facts in order, my dear," said Mrs. Roosevelt. "When you learned that Senator Gibson was dead, you decided to take your own life. You took an overdose of sleeping tablets, but fortunately—"

"I'm not so sure it was 'fortunately.' "

"Oh, my *dear!*" cried Mrs. Roosevelt. "Though it may not seem so at the moment, life is better . . . Life is— Believe me."

The First Lady glanced into the faces of all around her. The moment was awkward, painful.

Joanne Winthrop relieved the tension. "I won't try it again," she said. "I'm not very good at it."

"You were in love with Senator Gibson, weren't you?" asked Mrs. Roosevelt.

Joanne nodded. "Yes. And he was in love with me."

"I am sorry to have to mention this, dear, but Senator Gibson was a married man."

"We had plans," said Joanne simply.

"Can you tell us what they were?"

"He was going to divorce her. He had grounds. She's had

at least two love affairs. If he couldn't get the divorce, then we were going to do something else."

"Can you say what that was?"

"Well . . . He assumed that the divorce, with a lot of scandal, would make it impossible for him to be reelected. He supposed his career in the Senate was over. If he couldn't get a divorce, we were just going to go away. Probably to the Bahamas."

"Did he know you were pregnant?"

"Yes."

"Joanne," said Mrs. Roosevelt hesitantly, "I feel compelled to ask you an embarrassing question. Was Senator Gibson giving you money?"

"I'm not embarrassed about that," she said. "Yes, ma'am, he was giving me money. He gave me a regular allowance, also generous gifts of cash. That's how I was able to live in Washington after my father lost so much he cut me down to a hundred dollars a month. I told Vance I'd get a job, but he said no, he'd take care of me. I can't stay in Washington now. I'll have to go home to Boston and live with my parents."

"When did you last see Senator Gibson?"

Joanne closed her eyes. "About five or six hours before . . . He and I were together in his apartment that afternoon. When I heard on the radio that evening that he had been murdered, *I just couldn't bear it!*"

"Captain Kennelly will take you home, dear. If you should decide you want to stay in Washington, I imagine the President and I may be able to help you find work."

After Joanne Winthrop and Ed Kennelly left, Mrs. Roosevelt turned to Baines and said, "I don't detect a lie in what she said. Do you?"

Baines shook his head.

"What I detect is a tragedy," said the President.

"I saw no point in telling her that Constance Harrison, too, thought he was in love with her and her alone—or that he slept with Miss Mason also, and apparently with others. She's suffering enough, I think."

"It will come out in time," said Missy.

"I have a piece of information," said Baines.

"Don't let my shaking another round of drinks interrupt you," said the President, and he opened the silver cocktail shaker, poured out the dregs of his earlier martinis, and began to measure gin and vermouth.

"I spoke with Senator Truman this afternoon," said Baines. "He was at the table with Judge and Mrs. Harrison Wednesday evening. He confirms her story that she got up and left the table only after Senator Gibson left. But he added something else."

"This sounds ominous," said the President. "What did Harry have to add?"

"That Mrs. Harrison had also left the table about fifteen minutes before. That means she might have let someone in. She could have opened the locked door to the tunnel to the Treasury Building. The murderer could have been in the White House for a quarter of an hour, waiting for Senator Gibson to appear in the East Room."

"But how," asked the President, "would Mrs. Harrison or the person she let in know that Senator Gibson was coming to the East Room, or when?"

Missy laughed. "You missed your calling, Effdee," she chuckled. "You should have been a detective."

"As Sherlock Holmes so aptly and so repeatedly put it," said the President, "being a successful detective is simply a matter of applying iron logic to observed facts. I am simply asking, how would a murderer have known when to be where?"

"It is a remote possibility," said Mrs. Roosevelt, "but we cannot overlook the possibility that Mrs. Harrison, who had a long-standing intimate relationship with Senator Gibson, asked her to meet him in the East Room at such-and-such a time—to steal a kiss and perhaps a bit more. If she did not kill him herself, which jealousy might have driven her to do, she could have admitted someone else into the White House to—"

"Which assumes," said Missy, "that she knew the White House rather intimately."

"Her husband is descended from President Benjamin Harrison and President William Henry Harrison," said Baines. "She herself is descended from Merriweather Lewis. I believe the Hardings did not invite either of those families to the White House. *They* wouldn't have. Mrs. Harrison was first in the White House during the presidency of Theodore Roosevelt. She has been a guest here eight times since 1933."

X

When she left the West Sitting Hall that evening, the First Lady was driven to the Mayflower Hotel to attend a small, private—actually confidential—dinner with some leaders of the Democratic Party.

Although she tried to keep the matter secret, the truth was that Mrs. Roosevelt was in her own right one of the leaders of a faction within the Democratic Party. She had been so, actually, before her husband was elected President of the United States. During his illness and long recuperation, she had been active in New York state politics and had gained for herself a nationwide reputation for her support for liberal and humanitarian causes. This could have been a political liability for Governor Roosevelt during his 1932 campaign for the presidency, and it could very definitely have been a liability since; and so she had been at some pains to play down her own leadership role. She brought issues to the attention of the President. Daily she urged on him elements of her personal agenda, but she played a public role of loyal and supportive wife—and nothing more.

Even in that persona she had been subjected to vicious personal attacks. A story widely circulated—no one would claim credit for it—was that the President did not suffer paralysis from polio but from syphilis, which he had contracted from Mrs. Roosevelt, who in turn had contracted it from a black southern sharecropper with whom she'd long had an intimate relationship. There was an element on the fringe of the Republican Party who hated her more than they hated the President and who could think of no lie too cruel and outrageous to circulate. No adulteration of truth was too vindictive for the publisher of the Chicago *Tribune,* "Colonel" Bertie McCormick: a driveling, tiresome megalomaniac, yet the owner of a big newspaper. The columnist Westbrook Pegler had once been a friend, but he now used his column, called "George Spelvin, American," to excoriate the entire Roosevelt family. They could afford to laugh at Pegler though; his preachy, right-wing alter ego George Spelvin was about as relevant and influential, politically, as the Katzenjammer Kids.

In a private dining suite in the Mayflower, Mrs. Roosevelt found some of the guests already assembled: Harry Hopkins, Frances Perkins, Harold Ickes, Sidney Hillman of the Amalgamated Clothing Workers, and a man the First Lady found she was seeing more and more, Congressman Lyndon Johnson.

Absent from the meeting was the man whose name was on everyone's tongue. In testimony before the House Labor Committee, John L. Lewis, the fiery, outspoken president of the United Mine Workers, had stunned the committee and the nation by testifying—"The genesis of the current campaign against labor is not hard to find. It emanates from a labor-baiting, poker-playing, whisky-drinking evil old man whose name is Garner." Since Vice President Garner was the only major announced candidate for the 1940 Democratic nomination, Lewis's astonishing statement had electrified the kind of people who were at this meeting tonight.

Indeed, it was why Congressman Lyndon Johnson was present. Congressman Rayburn had prepared a statement and asked the senators and representatives from Texas to sign it. It denied that Garner drank or played poker and expressed the delegation's complete confidence in him. Of the entire delegation, only Johnson had refused to sign. Unofficially, he was the President's leader and spokesman in Texas.

Many southern Democrats had opposed the New Deal from the beginning. More were disenchanted with it now. The nomination of Vice President Garner, and his election as President of the United States, would return control of the Democratic Party to its old-time, old-line traditions.

"Have you seen the *Fortune* poll?" Sidney Hillman asked Mrs. Roosevelt.

"Yes, I have seen it," she said.

He referred to a public-opinion poll that said the President would be comfortably reelected if he ran—but that any other Democrat would go down in the face of a Republican landslide.

"I'd have liked Harry," said Sidney Hillman, nodding toward Harry Hopkins. "But I guess his health—"

"I am afraid Harry really can't run," she said. "He has been quite ill."

"Everything we stand for is at stake," said Hillman. "It's not just what's happening in Europe. Without the President, they'll beat us; and a coalition of Republicans and southern Democrats will dismantle everything that's been accomplished. We'll be put back to where we were when Herbert Hoover was President."

"I think some of what we've done is quite permanent and *can not* be dismantled," she said.

"You are optimistic. The President must run. The alternative is too horrible to contemplate."

Ed Kennelly sat down across the desk from Fire Marshal John Erwin.

"We're lucky the one family that was in the building got out alive," said Kennelly.

"Not exactly," said Erwin. "It wasn't luck. Somebody taped a note to a brick and tossed it through their living-room window. Here—"

He handed Kennelly the note. It read—

Git out quick. Big fire gonna bust out.

"Shortly," said Erwin, "a big fire did 'bust out.' A big fire that spread quick. There's no question but that it was arson. Professional job. He didn't want to risk a murder charge, so he warned the family. But he'd put enough gasoline and kerosine in the building to spread the fire all through, fast. The woman got her kids out fast, and she said she could smell gasoline in the hall as she hurried her kids out to the street."

"Anybody new on the list?" Kennelly asked.

"Nope."

"I guess I better check those guys," said Kennelly.

Charles Foster, city editor of the Washington *Post,* nodded and frowned, and a faint smile came over his face. "It's the most unusual request I've had in thirty years of newspapering, but I guess we ought to extend that much cooperation to the police."

"I'd be grateful," said Kennelly.

"Okay," said Foster. "You say you just want one copy?"

"Yes, sir. That's all I need."

Foster turned to his typewriter. "Let's see now— Oh. You *will* contact the woman and explain, won't you?"

"I will, definitely. She shouldn't ever hear of it, but I will talk to her, just in case."

*   *   *

A little before midnight, a uniformed officer cut his car in front of a car driven by Joseph Lavelle, who was trying to pull out of a parking place. Kennelly cut in behind him, and Lavelle was boxed.

"Hey! What is this? You can be a little more subtle. What's the beef?"

Kennelly faced the small, bald man. "Captain Ed Kennelly. Homicide. Seen the first edition of the *Post*, Joe?"

"No, I haven't. What should I see in the first edition of the *Post?*"

"Take a look," said Kennelly. He unfolded a newspaper and propped it up against the back of Lavelle's Plymouth, where the headlights from his own car shone on it. "Right here."

Kennelly tapped his finger on a front-page story. It read—

INFANT DIES IN ARSON FIRE
CHILD DIES IN TORCHED BUILDING

An eight-month-old infant died in a late-morning fire in a small apartment building on West Virginia Avenue. Mrs. Virginia Low, mother of the dead child, tearfully told fire investigators that she was warned that the fire was about to break out, that she ran out of the building with her older children, but that she was unable to return through the smoky flames to rescue the infant she had left in its crib in her bedroom.

Fire Marshal John Erwin said that, while the Fire Department will continue its investigation, he has referred the case to the District police, homicide division. He has no doubt, he said, that the fire was intentionally set, and the death of the infant makes the crime murder.

A large quantity of gasoline and kerosene had been used as "accelerants" to cause the fire to spread rapidly through the building.

Lavelle shook his head. "Why am I readin' this? What I got to do with it?"

"You're on a short list, Joe," said Kennelly. "We don't have many torches in Washington. Just a few. A short list."

"An' you got me on your list?"

"We've got you on the list. You did the job on Rizutto & Sons. You did time for it. You did time for the Wonder Bakery fire."

"True," said Lavelle. "But— Hey, you're from homicide, huh? Ask the fire marshal about me. Ask your own guys that work on arson cases. They'll tell ya. Okay, so I did two jobs and I'm on a list forever. But guys who know about me will tell ya. Nobody ever died in any fire I ever did. What's more, I never tossed gas around a place. Ask!"

"We'll ask while you sit in a cell," said Kennelly. He nodded to the uniformed officer. "Cuff him and take him in."

Kennelly found the second man on his list at home in his apartment, not very far from the building that had burned. He sat in a chair in his living room, alternately sucking oxygen from a tube that led to a cylinder and tobacco smoke from a Lucky Strike. He was dying of emphysema. It was too obvious. He couldn't be faking it. His wife said he had not been out of the apartment in six weeks, and Kennelly believed it.

Jerry Baines met him at two o'clock. They ate hotdogs and drank beer, then set out to find the third torch on the list.

They had word from the fire marshal's office that Rudy Ballou spent much of his time at a bar on Third Street N.E., where, together with many of its regular customers, he was welcome to drink illegally—after hours. Waldo's, the place was called. It was dark, but when Kennelly used the butt of his revolver to pound on the door, a man opened it.

"Who th' hell are you?"

"My name is Captain Edward Kennelly, chief of homicide, District police. Who the hell are you?"

"I jus' work here."

"Fine. You're doing your job; I'm doing mine. I'm coming in. Okay?"

The man shrugged. "I jus' work here."

"Who's in charge?"

"Bill Waldo. He's behind the bar."

Kennelly walked to the bar and showed his badge. "Captain Kennelly, homicide squad," he said. "I don't give a damn if you stay open after hours and sell illegally. That's somebody else's problem. But you withhold one iota of cooperation from me, I'll close you permanently."

Bill Waldo was a burly man, vaguely reminiscent of the cartoon character Roughhouse in "Popeye." He was rinsing glasses and drying them with his white apron. "I guess you would," he said. "So what's this cooperation I'm supposed to give you every iota of?"

"I'm looking for Rudy Ballou," said Kennelly.

Waldo shrugged. "That's him at the end of the bar." He smiled. "Rudy seems to have come into some luck. Got some money all of a sudden."

"Figures," said Kennelly.

"Can't sell you a drink, Captain," said Waldo. "It's after hours. Don't suppose that stops me from offering one on the house. You and your friend?"

"Gin on the rocks," said Kennelly. "My friends likes Scotch."

Waldo reached under the counter to come up with a bottle of Beefeater gin and a bottle of Black Label Scotch. "The good stuff," he said. "Not much call for it."

Kennelly raised his glass. "Rudy Ballou's a torch," he said.

"I wouldn't know," said Waldo. "I wouldn't be surprised, either."

Ballou sat on a bar stool at the end of the bar, conspicuously drunk, attended by a frowzy woman who might have been a blonde or brunette but had dyed her hair bright red with henna.

"He cadges drinks sometimes," said Waldo. "Broke. Then, like tonight, he's rolling in dough."

"You wouldn't know if he's a torch," said Kennelly. "Okay. We'll leave it at that. But if he just happened to be, is he any good at it?"

"Rumors," said Waldo. "When you work behind a bar, you hear everything. What I hear about Rudy Ballou is that he's crude but effective."

"He carrying a gun?" asked Kennelly.

"Be a big surprise to me if he is."

"Who's the broad?"

Waldo shrugged. "Hooker. He's been treatin' her like a lady. You can guess what that means."

Rudy Ballou vomited. He read the story on the front page of the *Post,* then suddenly he vomited. A policeman hosed him down and hosed the floor until the last of the stinking vomit went down the drain in the center of the floor.

Ballou was naked. He was chained to a heavy chair in the drunk tank in police headquarters. The other drunks had been moved to other cells, and he sat alone in the middle of the tank, hooked to the chair with two pairs of handcuffs. He was a grossly fat figure, yet a little man, not more than five feet five. He was thirty-nine years old but looked fifty-five or sixty. His face was red and puffy. His pale blue eyes bulged.

"Fellas . . ." he muttered. "I gotta pee."

"So pee," said Kennelly.

Ballou closed his eyes for a moment, then let his urine go. The uniformed officer rinsed him off with the hose. The water was cold, and Ballou shuddered.

"What you got on me? What you got on me?"

"A dead baby," said Kennelly, tapping his finger on the only copy of the Washington *Post* that said anything about a child dying in the fire on West Virginia Avenue.

Ballou shook his head. "I didn't do that. I didn't have anything to do with that."

"Rudy . . ." said Kennelly quietly, with mock patience. "You wanta stick with that story? You got one chance, Rudy. Just one chance. You give us a full confession. Otherwise—" Kennelly made a gesture suggesting hanging. "You wanta give us a statement?"

The statement typed up by a police secretary and signed by Rudy Ballou at five A.M. read—

I, Rudolph Ballou, having been fully informed of my rights under the law and the Constitution, and being under no compulsion or threat, do make the following statement of my own free will.

I do freely confess that on June 12, 1940, I did set a fire in a certain building on West Virginia Avenue, the street number being now unknown to me. I threw a brick through the window of the only apartment in the building where anyone seemed to be present, attaching a note that the building was about to be set on fire. I used gasoline and kerosene to "accelerate" the fire—that is, to cause it to spread rapidly and totally destroy the building and its contents before the fire department could arrive to extinguish the fire.

For this crime I was paid the sum of one thousand dollars ($1,000.00) by a man previously unknown to me, who came to my place of residence and offered to pay me this amount to set the fire. He told me his name was Richard Blair. I have no way to verify that. He paid me one hundred dollars ($100.00) at about ten o'clock in the morning and nine hundred dollars ($900.00) about two o'clock in the afternoon. Both payments were in cash, in fifty dollar ($50.00) bills.

Richard Blair did not state any reason why he wanted the building burned, except to demand from me an assurance that the fire would spread so rapidly and would be so destructive that nothing in the nature of papers or documents would survive. I so assured him and therefore used a far greater quantity of "accelerants" than I would have used in any other circumstance.

I fully believed before I lit the fire that every person had left the building.

I give this statement of my free will, being under no restraint or compulsion, and do certify that the facts above stated are true.

Rudolph Ballou

Among the possessions found in Ballou's clothes when he was arrested at Waldo's Bar was a wallet containing fourteen fifty-dollar bills. They bore distinct fingerprints, and when those were lifted they were carried to the F.B.I. fingerprint records file, at six in the morning on June 13.

"Bills circulate, Captain. They get all crumpled. It's unusual to be able to lift prints off them. But damned if your boys didn't."

"Some of the bills were new and crisp," said Kennelly.

"You got bingo on three of these prints," said the F.B.I. technician. "Here are the names and records. Good luck, Captain."

"Thanks," said Kennelly.

"If you don't mind my asking, Captain, when did you last get an hour's sleep?"

"You believe twenty-six hours ago? The question is, when am I *gonna* get an hour's sleep? The answer is, right now."

*   *   *

On fine days, Bernard Baruch liked to sit on a bench in Lafayette Park. He read the newspapers there, marked up letters and memoranda, and sometimes met with people. He preferred that setting to any indoor office.

Mrs. Roosevelt could not go over and sit in Lafayette Park. Even with Secret Service protection, she would have been interrupted constantly. So she and Baruch sat on a bench facing the White House rose garden.

"Naturally," said Baruch, "no one wanted to disclose any information. The two banks . . . the accountants. One does, though, have certain friends and resources." He smiled and lifted his eyebrows. "In any event I was able to get some interesting information about the financial status of Senator and Mrs. Gibson."

"I am grateful," said Mrs. Roosevelt. The day was warm, and she was wearing a simple white linen dress with white shoes. "I regret the necessity of having to snoop into other people's affairs, but I suspect you may have learned something significant."

"Amelia Gibson inherited roughly three-and-a-half-million dollars from her father. She was already married to Vance Gibson at the time. He was a prosperous lawyer. They had kept their funds and investments in joint accounts, and when she inherited her fortune she continued the practice."

"So he had access to everything?"

Baruch nodded. "He ran for the Senate in 1934 and was elected. When they moved to Washington, they transferred all their accounts to Washington banks. Her money was commingled with his, and so were her investment accounts. The only thing she owned exclusively is vast acreage in Idaho: her father's ranches. The land was left to her, and she never deeded half to her husband."

"Would you say he was a wealthy man in his own right?" asked Mrs. Roosevelt.

"He had done very well as a lawyer. He had inherited a

little. He had a very respectable estate of his own—though nothing like hers. Anyway, they spent nearly a quarter of a million on that Virginia estate—that is, on purchasing it and remodeling. Not counting the Idaho land, they were jointly worth something like four million dollars."

"Mrs. Gibson thinks he seriously diminished the estate in the last year."

"He did, very definitely."

"By bad investments?"

"No. By withdrawals. Beginning in November of 1939 and continuing until his death, he withdrew nearly a million dollars, mostly by selling stocks and bonds and transferring the cash away from their brokerage account. He withdrew fifty thousand dollars last Wednesday morning. In cash. There were a few other cash withdrawals, none as big as that. The other withdrawals can be traced and presumably recovered, at least in part."

Mrs. Roosevelt sighed and shook her head. "Miss Winthrop says he was planning on leaving Mrs. Gibson and going away, perhaps to the Bahamas."

"What about his reelection? Was he giving up his seat in the Senate?"

"Yes. Miss Winthrop believes he was deeply in love with her. If you met Joanne, you'd know why. She is a lovely girl."

"I have met Miss Winthrop," said Baruch. "She is indeed a lovely girl. One can understand the attraction. She would have brought grace and elegance to his life, more than he could ever hope to have from his wife."

"I don't see much grace and elegance in her encouraging a man to run away from his wife and come live with her, whether they could be married or not," said Mrs. Roosevelt. "He married Amelia for her money, of course. Then he wanted to take *her* money and run off with a girl seventeen years younger. Does Amelia Gibson know how much is missing from the accounts?"

"Yes. She has been inquiring. In fact, on Friday, two days after his death, she ordered the accounting firm to start tracing the funds. Because the funds were transferred by checks on the brokerage account, they may well be able to discover where the money went. I would assume it went to other banks, probably in a different name—maybe in the Bahamas."

Mrs. Roosevelt frowned. "Fifty thousand dollars in cash, on the day he was killed. I wonder where that went."

Ed Kennelly whistled. "Fifty thousand!"

"Could it have been in the apartment?" asked Mrs. Roosevelt.

"We didn't search thoroughly," said Kennelly. "We were looking for some fingerprints, that's all." He turned to Baines. "Ohhh, boy! Could Lena Madison have got it?"

"It would have had to be accidentally if she did," said Mrs. Roosevelt. "How could she have known it was there? Surely the Senator wouldn't have left that much money lying about. It would have been hidden, and the maid would not have found it unless she knew it was there and searched for it."

"Someone else was in the apartment after the Senator withdrew the money," said Baines. "Joanne Winthrop."

"We don't know the money ever reached the apartment," said the First Lady. "He could have done something else with it."

"Could it have been on him when he was killed?" asked Kennelly.

"That is highly doubtful," said Mrs. Roosevelt. "Even if it were all in thousand-dollar bills, it would have been quite bulky. And I doubt it could have been in thousand-dollar bills. I should imagine few cashiers have that many of those in their cash drawers."

"Then what did he do with it?" asked Baines.

"Fifty thousand dollars, fifty thousand possibilities," said Mrs. Roosevelt. "This could turn the investigation into a farce."

They were sitting on the bench in the rose garden, where she had met with Baruch. The fine day was soon going to be interrupted by a thunderstorm. It was building to the south and west, and already they could hear thunder. Mrs. Roosevelt had sometimes wondered if Abraham Lincoln, standing on the lawn south of the White House, could have heard the thunder of artillery during the two battles along Bull Run. She had little doubt that he had, but she could not remember having specifically read anywhere that he did.

"I've got some new information," said Kennelly. "About another side of the case. We arrested the arsonist who burned out Laura Mason's apartment. He confessed. He's not a very good torch, not very professional. But he's a lot more professional than the man who paid him to do the job. That man paid him a thousand dollars in twenty-dollar bills. A few of the bills were new. When he counted them off, he left his fingerprints on them."

"So you know who it is?" asked Baines.

Kennelly nodded. "He's a Washington insurance agent by the name of Jack Gordon. The F.B.I. has his fingerprints on file because when he was in the army in 1917–18, he worked at the Army Ordnance Depot. I haven't had him picked up. I bet anything it's going to lead us to McGinnis. I thought I'd better mention that. Congressman McGinnis won't cave in easy. He'll be tough."

"If he murdered Senator Gibson," said Mrs. Roosevelt, "or conspired in the murder, then we have to pursue him, no matter who he is or how tough. But you should be certain of your evidence. To charge him and then not be able to substantiate the charge would be a disaster."

"The torch is named Rudy Ballou," said Kennelly. "He confessed, but he won't make a very good witness."

"The fingerprints are your best evidence now, I suppose,"

said the First Lady. "But currency circulates, and there must be other fingerprints on those bills."

"Right," said Kennelly. "We found five bills on Ballou that had Gordon's fingerprints on them. The best example has just four sets of prints on it: Ballou and Gordon and two more. We figure one of the other two sets is a bank teller. The big question, I suppose, is whether or not Gordon will confess when Ballou identifies him and he sees we have the fingerprints."

"The big question, actually," said Mrs. Roosevelt, "is whether or not Mr. Gordon leads us to someone else. Is it likely that he himself had any reason to want Senator Gibson dead? I imagine not. He was working for someone else, I should imagine. We must find out who."

The President sat in the Oval Office, eating his lunch—a tuna-salad sandwich and an apple—and talking to Harry Hopkins and Secretary of State Cordell Hull.

"There are no newspapers in Paris," he said. "The last ones were printed Monday. The printers have stayed at their presses and run off thousands of posters that are being put up all over the city. Paris has been declared an open city. The population is being told not to resist the Germans."

"There's not a damned thing we can do about it," said Hopkins.

"There was a year ago," said the President bitterly.

XI

Rudy Ballou, subdued in the blue denims of the D.C. jail, stood inside a darkened room, where the only light came from the room beyond, through a two-way mirror. Joe Lavelle, in the same uniform, stood beside him. The two torches were handcuffed together. They stared at a lineup in the room beyond the mirror.

"Number 3," said Ballou quietly.

"I never seen none of those guys," said Lavelle.

"Think careful, Joe," said Kennelly. "Think . . . careful."

"I don't . . . I don't. I never seen none of those guys."

"Number 4?" asked Kennelly.

Lavelle shook his head emphatically. "Never seen him."

"That's the cop that arrested you last night," said Kennelly.

"Well . . . hell. He's out of uniform."

"Rudy says Number 3."

"I don't care. I never seen Number 3."

"Okay, Rudy. Who is he?"

"Richard Blair," said Rudy Ballou.

* * *

"One of the most respectable citizens of our city," said Lloyd Nordstrom, who had appeared at headquarters while Kennelly was with the two prisoners at the lineup. He had introduced himself as attorney for Jack Gordon. "It is an outrage, Captain, that a man of his reputation and character should—"

"Counselor," Kennelly interrupted firmly. "Your client just stood in a lineup and was positively identified as the man who paid a known and self-confessed arsonist a thousand dollars to torch an apartment building on West Virginia Avenue."

"And you take the word of this . . . *felon?*"

"I might not, except that I have fingerprint evidence that puts the icing on the cake."

Nordstrom was a tall, self-important blond man, with yellow hair combed meticulously across his head and forehead. His supercilious blue eyes regarded Kennelly as though he had just discovered something smelly on his shoe. "I want to talk with my client," he said.

Kennelly nodded. "You can talk to him right now."

"I demand his release. This is a formal demand."

"I refuse to release him. This is a formal refusal."

"Just how long do you propose to hold him?"

"Forty-eight hours. After which I must either prefer charges or release him. You can advise him the charge will be filed."

Jack Gordon sat disconsolately on the cot in a cell. He had not been put into the denim uniform but sat in his shirt-sleeves. The jacket of his tan, double-breasted suit lay folded on the foot of the cot, with his necktie. He had been allowed to keep his cigarettes and was smoking a Wings.

Kennelly walked up to the bars of the cell. "Mr. Gordon," he said. "Ed Kennelly, captain in charge of the homicide squad."

"My God, there's no *homicide!*"

"Oh, yes. In the fire," said Kennelly. "Felony murder—a death caused in the course of committing arson."

Gordon rose and came to the bars. "I've never been in jail before in my life," he said miserably.

"When a man has a lawyer," said Kennelly, "we never suggest he go against his lawyer's advice. Mr. Nordstrom probably told you, though, that I've got evidence and plan to charge you with felony murder—arson."

"It's got to be a mistake," said Gordon.

"You figure I should be looking for a man named Richard Blair," said Kennelly.

Gordon turned away and walked to the rear wall of his cell, then returned to the bars. "What do you want?" he asked.

"You didn't care if that building burned down," said Kennelly. "There was nothing in it for you. You hired Rudy Ballou to do it for somebody else. How'd you know to contact Rudy, anyway?"

"He torched a building I'd insured," said Gordon. "And got away with it. I figured if he was smart enough to do that—"

"They call you 'Flash,' don't they?"

Gordon walked over and popped his burning cigarette butt into the toilet. "Some people do," he said.

"I can't make deals," said Kennelly. "But I figure you've been suckered. Hell, you weren't even smart, Flash. You're looking at a life sentence, and I bet you did it as a favor, didn't get a dollar for what you did."

Gordon clung to the bars, and suddenly he sobbed. "What's going to happen to my wife and kids?" he wept.

"Like I said, I can't make deals. I can tell a judge a man got suckered and then cooperated. Let me guess. Lloyd Nordstrom isn't your lawyer at all. He came here to tell you to keep your mouth shut. He could care less how much time you do."

Gordon nodded.

"I suppose I can set up a little conference with a United States attorney."

"I made the inquiry you asked for," Mrs. Roosevelt said to Kennelly. "I telephoned Attorney General Jackson and asked him to have one of his people check the name of Lloyd Nordstrom. His firm is Washington counsel for several major insurance companies. Besides that, he is a lobbyist for the insurance industry."

"Somebody is scared, then," said Kennelly. "They want to torch Laura Mason's apartment. The first thing they do is get a local insurance agent to hire the torch. Then, when he gets caught, they send one of their most notorious lawyers to— Well . . . To threaten him, is what Nordstrom did."

"If they were being clever," said Mrs. Roosevelt, "they would have left levels of anonymity between themselves and the man you call a 'torch.' Am I right?"

"That's exactly right," said Kennelly.

They were settled into a routine fixed over the past week: they met in Mrs. Roosevelt's study at about the same time when the President was enjoying his cocktails in the West Sitting Hall. She drank tea and ate two or three finger sandwiches. Lest Kennelly and Baines be disappointed they were not outside at the President's cocktail hour, she ordered gin and Scotch for them.

"You say Mr. Gordon gave a statement?"

"He's pitiful, ma'am. He thinks—and he's right—that he's been used. He's desperate. He was allowed to make a telephone call to his wife, to tell her he's in jail; and he cried so much he could hardly talk to her."

"Should we feel sympathy?" asked the First Lady.

"Well— Let me summarize his statement."

"Please do," she said, extending a plate of finger sandwiches toward him.

Kennelly chose a ham and cheese sandwich. "It's like this," he said. "Most insurance agencies are honest—if by definition there is any such thing as honesty in selling insurance. But remember what Jerry told us about the notary bonds fraud in Ohio? Well, there's a lot of fraud like that. For example, Jack Gordon wrote a lot of insurance on buildings that didn't exist, or that were ruined shells. Here's the way it works—Gordon as agent writes a fire policy on a building that doesn't exist. X.Y.Z. Company pays premiums on that insurance. A.B.C. Insurance Company is the insurer, but A.B.C. only takes, say, ten percent of the premium, because there's no exposure, no liability. So why would X.Y.Z. Company want to pay those premiums? It doesn't. But its directors and accountants don't know that's what it's doing. This premium disappears into the company's overall insurance expense."

"But where does the money go?" asked Mrs. Roosevelt.

"Gordon takes some. Lobbyists for the insurance industry take some, which is one way the industry funds its very costly lobbying efforts. And somebody else gets some. Like maybe Congressman Howard McGinnis."

"Do we know that? Was Congressman McGinnis involved?"

"We don't know that yet. And it may not be true, either. But that's the kind of fraud Senator Vance Gibson had been trying to stop—which was reason enough to want to kill him."

"The links in this chain stop short of Congressman McGinnis," said Mrs. Roosevelt.

"Well, there's one more link. Torching the apartment building wasn't Gordon's idea, and the cash he paid Rudy Ballou wasn't his either. He got both the idea and the money from a woman. Her name is Muriel Griffith. Gordon tried to be vague about her. I figure she's no casual acquaintance."

"You mean . . . ?"

"Oh. No. Business. I got the impression that she's the link

between Gordon and the brains behind the fraud. I don't think he's got the smarts or the guts to have figured it out."

"A dangerous assumption," said Baines.

"Well, there's something else he hasn't got," said Kennelly. "The contacts. Until three or four years ago, he was strictly a nuts-and-bolts insurance agent. Sold some automobile insurance, some fire insurance, some life insurance. Made a decent living but was no star. Then suddenly he's doin' a whole lot better. And that's because somebody made him a front man for a lot of fraud."

"Did he confess this?" asked the First Lady.

"Not in those terms," said Kennelly dryly. "But, listen. Jack 'Flash' Gordon is so miserable in jail and so afraid that he'll confess anything we ask."

"We only want the truth."

"I mean the truth."

"Anyway," said Mrs. Roosevelt. "Who is Muriel Griffith, and where do you find her?"

"Gordon describes her as a tall, dark-haired woman with a long, thin face. When I was sitting in McGinnis's office I noticed a picture on the wall, of a group of people, standing on the Capitol steps, it looked like. One of the people was a tall, dark-haired woman with a long, thin face. I'd like to get my hands on that picture and show it to Gordon. Then I'd like to know who she is."

"A picture on the wall of Congressman McGinnis's office," said Mrs. Roosevelt with a smile, shaking her head. "A scavenger hunt! I wonder if the Congressman is still in his office."

"Mrs. Roosevelt! What an honor!" gushed McGinnis, astounded to find the First Lady in the anteroom. "Come in! Come in!"

She entered his office and sat down. She was wearing the white linen dress she had worn all day, only she had added a white straw hat and gloves. It was only a little after six, and the sun still shone brightly through the office windows.

"I was on the Hill, paying a few calls," she said, "and it occurred to me that even though you have been here since 1935 we have never met. I try to make it a point to meet all the senators and representatives, and I am wondering how we happened to have missed each other."

McGinnis grinned. "Well, I *am* a Republican, ma'am," he said.

"For the purposes of polite social contact, that makes no difference," she said.

She had located the photograph Kennelly wanted. It was one of a dozen framed pictures on his office wall. The walls of congressional offices were typically decorated with pictures of people shaking hands or facing the camera in small groups. She noticed a picture of McGinnis shaking hands with John Bricker, Governor of Ohio. In another he was shaking hands with Wendell Willkie, the maverick Indiana utilities lawyer who was seeking the Republican nomination.

She guessed the group picture with the tall woman in the center was a photo of McGinnis's office staff. If she was the Muriel Griffith mentioned by Jack Gordon, here was the link between McGinnis and the fire.

"Warm for this time of year," said McGinnis. It was a weak essay at conversation. The man was authentically dumbfounded to find the First Lady sitting in front of his desk.

Mrs. Roosevelt coughed. "It is indeed," she said. She coughed again. "Excuse me. And, this being Washington, it's going to get much warmer."

"Yes. I suppose this city is a little oppressive to all of us who are accustomed to a very different climate."

Mrs. Roosevelt coughed still again. "Please do excuse me," she said. "I think I've swallowed a gnat."

"Let me get you a drink of cold water," he said.

"Oh, yes, thank you."

On her way in, she had noticed that the water cooler was in a far corner of the anteroom. That was why she had pretended to cough. Congressman McGinnis would not be able to see what she was about to do.

She reached into her purse and quickly pulled out a Minox camera. The tiny stainless-steel camera, only a little more than three inches long, less than an inch wide and less than an inch thick, used 16 mm film. Its optics were so nearly perfect that clear small prints could be made from its little negatives. She had rehearsed what she must do and knew that she must step up to within two feet of the photograph on the wall, make one shot, change the exposure setting and make another, change it again and shoot a third time. She had half a minute or less to do it, but that was enough.

When McGinnis returned with a paper cone of water, the First Lady was standing in front of his pictures. The camera was deep in her purse. "Oh, thank you so much!" she said. She drank the water. "That's Governor Bricker, isn't it?"

"Yes," said McGinnis. "A fine man, John. A man that handsome is going to be a candidate for President someday."

She sat down again. "Well, tell me, Congressman McGinnis, what do you think of this week's events in France?"

Congressman McGinnis didn't know what was happening in France at that hour, but the President did. Radio traffic between French and German officers had been monitored and secretly transmitted to London and Washington. The Germans were demanding that military stores in the city be left intact, not destroyed. They demanded that the bridges over the Seine, particularly those that carried utility lines, were not to be destroyed. Citizens were to remain in their homes on Friday and Saturday.

Paris was an open city. It was also a silent one. The métro was not running. Civilian radio stations were mute. Stores and businesses were closed. The streets were all but abandoned.

The President listened to the grim radio reports. He took a call from the State Department. Then he told Missy to put a stack of records on the player. Frustrated and discouraged, he didn't want to hear anything but music.

The most meticulous film developing in Washington was done at the Bureau of Printing and Engraving. When she left Capitol Hill, Mrs. Roosevelt went directly there, where she met Baines and Kennelly and a technician who had been asked to come in after hours to process an important piece of film.

The man had never worked with one of the tiny 16-mm film cartridges before, and there were anxious moments in the darkroom as he tried to open it and remove the film for developing. After a while he shut the cartridge in a light-tight box and asked for another cartridge, one with unexposed film in it. He opened that cartridge in the light and saw how to do it and how to get the film out without damaging it.

He didn't have a tank for 16-mm film, either; but he put clips on both ends of the film and immersed it in one of the big tanks in which the Bureau's film plates were developed. The key was fine-grain developing. Fine-grain chemistry was slow, and it was almost half an hour before the technician could hold the film up to the light and announce that there were clear images on the film.

While the film was drying, he cut a paper mask to be inserted between the glass plates in the enlarger. An hour and a quarter after Mrs. Roosevelt delivered the film, she stood behind the technician in the darkroom and watched a positive image emerge on a piece of photographic paper.

As she had asked, he had cropped the picture so as to show the woman alone.

"Success, ma'am," said the technician. "I'd say that's about as clear a picture as you could get with a camera that small."

She offered to pay him for his time. He told her he would rather she sent him an autographed picture of herself. She promised he would receive one—and one from the President, too.

The woman in the photograph was tall. Her hair looked unnaturally dark, as if it were dyed. Her face was thin. Her cheeks looked caved in; there were shadows beneath her cheekbones. Her thin lower lip was pushed out by protruding upper teeth.

Jack Gordon gripped a cell bar with his left hand and the little photograph with his right. "That's her. That's Muriel," he said.

Kennelly took the picture back and handed him a second print, this one not cropped to eliminate the other people in the group. "You know any of those others?" he asked.

"My God! That's Howard McGinnis!"

"You know McGinnis?" Kennelly asked.

"Well . . . sure. He's an important spokesman for the insurance industry, in the Congress."

"The man behind some of those sweet deals you've had," said Kennelly.

"Well . . . I wouldn't want to say that."

"You'd better say somethin', if you want to avoid a life term."

The First Lady and Jerry Baines had waited in Kennelly's car while he went in and showed Gordon the pictures. Now, they had agreed, they would go to dinner, where they could review the investigation to now.

They ate at Harvey's. Director Hoover and his assistant Tolson were on their way out as Mrs. Roosevelt and her two friends came in. Hoover was elaborately deferential and asked Kennelly if he'd had all the cooperation he needed from the F.B.I. fingerprint lab. Kennelly assured him he had.

The management could not adequately express its pleasure at having the First Lady at one of their tables. They were hardly seated when a bottle of vintage French champagne arrived, compliments of the house.

"It *is* better than New York State champagne, isn't it?" said Mrs. Roosevelt.

Baines, who had taken a sip of the champagne, stared at the bubbles rising in his glass. "There is no such thing as New York State champagne," he said.

"Well . . . sparkling white wine, then, to put a fine point on the matter."

"To be altogether frank, ma'am—and probably too frank—New York State sparkling wine is enough to make a vintner vomit."

She smiled. "The vomiting vintner, Mr. Baines, does not have to pay the White House bills."

"Enjoy," said Kennelly. "It's on the house."

Mrs. Roosevelt lifted her glass. "To success," she said. "We pulled off something of a *coup* tonight, did we not?"

"We did indeed," said Kennelly with a broad grin. "Congressman McGinnis is in very deep trouble."

She nodded, then frowned. "We've connected him to the arson. I'm afraid, though, we've made no better connection to the murder of Senator Gibson."

"I hate to admit it," said Baines, "but we aren't much closer than we were last Wednesday night to knowing who killed Senator Gibson."

"Let's think about Mrs. Harrison," said the First Lady. "She left her table twice— Incidentally, Mr. Baines, I don't recall how far apart were the table where the Gibsons sat and the table where the Harrisons sat."

"Three tables apart," said Baines.

Mrs. Roosevelt nodded and for a moment frowned thoughtfully. "We have assumed," she said, "that someone let someone in. That may well have been a gross error. Isn't it really more likely that someone already inside the White House committed the crime?"

"And that someone," said Kennelly, "does not have to be someone who was in the State Dining Room."

"We've identified just four people who left their tables within the few minutes when the Senator was killed," said Baines. "Congressman Carl Vinson, Mrs. Dirksen, Mrs. Harrison, and of course Mrs. Gibson. An unlikely group of suspects."

"Two of them had motive," said Mrs. Roosevelt. "Mrs. Harrison may have discovered that she had been betrayed. Mrs. Gibson didn't have to discover—she knew—that Senator Gibson was looting their joint accounts."

"Let me ask a question," said Kennelly. "What would have happened the night of the State Dinner if a beautiful young woman, beautifully dressed, dripping with jewelry, came to the door and said she had been invited to the state dinner but had come without her invitation?"

Baines drew a breath. "She'd probably get in," he said. "Our security is tighter since the war broke out in Europe, but there's still the awful tradition that the White House is a public building. Anyway, dressed like you say— You're thinking of Joanne Winthrop."

"Or Brenda Frelinghuysen," said Kennelly. "Just a thought."

"Following your thought," said Mrs. Roosevelt, "I suppose you surmise that the Senator had broken off with Miss Winthrop that afternoon, maybe gave her the $50,000 he had withdrawn that morning, and told her to take it and rear their child with it. She killed him. Then, knowing she was bound to be discovered, she went home and tried to kill herself."

"It's easily checked," said Baines. "We'll simply ask the staff on duty at the door that night if they admitted a charming young woman who couldn't produce her invitation."

Kennelly smiled at Mrs. Roosevelt. "Using one of your favorite words again—'fanciful.' "

"In any event," said the First Lady, "I would like to know what became of the $50,000."

"All right," said Kennelly. "Talking about Joanne Winthrop, we're still talking about someone who entered the White House that evening. I think it's time to concentrate more on people we know were there, who were legitimately inside."

"My mind has been focused on that for some time," said Mrs. Roosevelt. "It persists in leading me to a conclusion I don't want to reach."

"And what is that?" asked Baines.

"I'd rather not say. I'd rather the two of you examined the facts and came to the conclusion independently."

"What facts?" Kennelly asked. "We've been staring at the facts for a week."

"For a week, almost, we've overlooked a fact that could have a major impact. *I've* overlooked it. I don't think either one of you knew about it."

Kennelly grinned. "Can't solve a case on facts we don't have," he said.

"All right. I didn't see the possible significance of the fact when it came to my attention," she said. "This is the fact— On Wednesday evening one of the waiters became ill. Actually, he became staggering drunk and eventually lost consciousness briefly. It seems—though I didn't know this—that some of the personnel make a point of emptying the half-empty wine glasses as they carry them back to the kitchen." She smiled faintly at Baines. "Even this colored waiter told me our wine is nauseating. For twenty-three years he has sampled the wine in glasses he was carrying back to the kitchen. That night it made him violently ill. He swore he didn't drink more than usual."

"A Mickey Finn!" cried Kennelly.

Mrs. Roosevelt nodded. "I've begun to wonder if— Well . . . Here's another fanciful scenario. When Senator Gibson left the table, he said he was ill. He was. He had sipped champagne that had something in it. Because he didn't like the champagne, he didn't drink much. But he drank enough to make him nauseous. And weak. *And weak.*"

"And being weak—" Baines began to say.

"Anyone would have been strong enough to cut his throat. Mrs. Harrison or Mrs. Gibson could have killed him."

"Exactly," said Mrs. Roosevelt.

"We didn't have an autopsy performed," said Kennelly. "That was a big mistake."

"Not only that," said Mrs. Roosevelt. "Not only was the body cremated. The ashes were scattered over the waters of Bull Run. And the urn was thrown into the water."

"So we could never prove—"

"Maybe," said Mrs. Roosevelt. "There might be a chance. It depends on what laboratories can do. Actually, we have a very considerable sample of Senator Gibson's blood. Mrs. Gibson's gown was soaked with it. I got a great deal of it on mine. Those two dresses haven't been disposed of. I shoved them into a carton and just haven't gotten around to having that carton removed. The fact is, I've been reluctant to ask a maid to carry away such a grisly thing. Anyway, they're here."

"For a Mickey to knock a man out," said Kennelly, "the stuff has to get into his blood and go to his brain."

"The question," said the First Lady, "is whether a laboratory can detect traces of a poison in week-old dried blood."

"The answer is yes," said Kennelly.

XII

Before turning off the light in her bedroom that Thursday night, Mrs. Roosevelt had listened to her shortwave radio for a quarter of an hour. She had tried to pick up a broadcast from Paris, but she could find no signal from Radio Paris. She listened to the BBC. The news was tragic.

She woke at 5:00 A.M. and switched the radio on again. With tears on her cheeks, she rang Hick's room on the telephone and asked Hick to come down. The two women, Lorena Hickock and the First Lady, sat in the bedroom as the sun rose higher and filled the room with morning light, and listened to the news.

An official at the Swedish consulate had somehow managed to make telephone connection with Zurich, from where BBC technicians relayed the call to England, where it went out on the North American Service.

"At dawn this morning, June 14, 1940, German soldiers marched into Paris. The first troops to enter the city have been identified as the Ninth Division, Army Group B, under command of General Fedor von Bock. In mid-morning, General von Bock held a review of these troops on the Place de la Concorde. Other units, described as soldiers of the Eighth and Twenty-eighth Divisions, marched through the Arch of Triumph and down the Champs Elysées.

"The city is quiet. I have heard not a single shot. The German soldiers seem perfectly disciplined. They appear to be jubilant young men, surprised by their victory. No complaints of looting have reached this consulate.

"An hour ago, standing on the roof and watching through binoculars, I witnessed a sight that must have chilled the heart of every citizen of France. I watched the German swastika flag raised atop the Eiffel Tower."

Two hours later the President read a transcript of the same broadcast. It was a highlight of a body of documents brought to him as soon as he picked up his telephone and notified the switchboard that he was awake. As he read each he handed it to Missy. He put the papers aside in three sorting piles she had established. From time to time the President told her to take a note. She had her shorthand pad and a pencil at hand and had so far made fourteen notes.

The most difficult communication the President had before him that morning was a desperate plea from Paul Reynaud, literally begging him to ask the Congress to declare war on Germany. He reminded the President of how the United States had come to the aid of France in 1917—of how France had helped the American colonies in their war to gain independence from Great Britain.

"The damned Congress won't declare war," the President muttered, to himself as much as to Missy. "Even if it did, we couldn't save France this time."

As he looked at the newspapers, even on this morning the isolationist press was demanding what it called "calm." The red-black-white swastika flag of Naziism flew from the Eiffel Tower, and the midwestern newspapers called for "calm."

"I'll want to speak to Henry Stimson this morning," said the President. "I'm going to have to have a strong and effective Secretary of War."

Jerry Baines sat down at Mrs. Nesbitt's desk in the house-keeper's office. He had before him a diagram of the tables as they had been set up in the State Dining Room last Wednesday evening.

"Okay now, Sam," he said to Sam Carter, the waiter who had become ill that evening, "point out to me which tables you handled that night."

The waiter pointed to two tables. "Thish yere," he said. "And thish yere."

One of the tables he had pointed to was the table where Senator and Mrs. Vance Gibson had sat.

A check of the staff rosters of the members of the House of Representatives had discovered on Congressman McGinnis's staff only two women who could be "Muriel Griffith"—both of them from Columbus, Ohio, one named Claudia Jones, the other Frieda Schneider. Kennelly sent cars to both their homes, to wait for the women to come out on their way to Capitol Hill. The officers had photographs of "Muriel Griffith." Claudia Jones was not Muriel Griffith. Frieda Schneider was. They arrested Frieda Schneider.

Protesting volubly but visibly frightened, Frieda Schneider stood in a lineup. Jack Gordon identified her, positively. He picked her out of a group of six women: two prostitutes, a shoplifter, a drunk, a secretary at police head-quarters, and herself.

Kennelly sat with her in an interrogation room. "You're what we sometimes call the bag woman, aren't you, Miss Schneider? You carry the money."

"I don't know what you're talking about," said Frieda

174   ELLIOTT ROOSEVELT

Schneider sullenly. She was the woman from the photograph, which had portrayed her perfectly. Her hair was dull
black, as if she had rubbed it with powdered charcoal. Her
cheeks were hollow under her high cheekbones, and she had
reddened them a little with rouge. "I don't even know what
a bag woman is."

"Let's say we're talking about two things," said Kennelly.
"You delivered the money that paid for the torching of the
apartment building on West Virginia Avenue. I've got you
cold on that one, lady. We don't even need to talk about it.
A child died in that fire, and we'll be holding you for the
grand jury on a charge of felony murder."

Her eyes widened. "Holding me? You mean you're going
to put me *in jail?*"

He nodded. "First stop on the road to the women's reformatory, life sentence. Arson. Serious charge, murder."

"I . . . I didn't do anything!"

"You delivered to Flash Gordon his orders to torch the
building on West Virginia Avenue. You gave him the address. You gave him the thousand dollars he used to pay the
torch. He's confessed to all of that."

"Well, it's his word against mine," she said weakly, not
convinced she was helping herself.

"The case against you doesn't hang on his word alone.
Some of the bills were new, and when you counted them off,
you left your fingerprints on them. Those bills wound up in
the hands of the confessed torch. The case is closed, Miss
Schneider. You go from here to a jail cell, from there to a
reformatory cell. Oh . . . would you like Mr. Nordstrom for
your lawyer?"

"She gave a statement," Kennelly told Mrs. Roosevelt on the
telephone. "I can almost feel sorry for her. She comes from
a city where anything can be fixed if your name is
Schneider. She simply can't believe she's locked up. She

broke down the same way Gordon did. I'm having her watched, for fear she'll do something to herself."

"What did she confess to?"

"She has been McGinnis's bag woman, which is what she was in Columbus. It's a full confession. She collected money from Gordon and others, for premiums paid for insurance that did not expose the insurers to any risk. He had done it in Columbus, and he brought the racket here, where being a congressman made it a whole lot easier. Many of the insurance companies are anxious to do something for a congressman who talks for them like Charlie McCarthy talks for Edgar Bergen. All the money was in cash. She carried it in a valise. This time she delivered a thousand dollars in cash to Gordon, to use to pay the torch. They didn't have a thousand in cash in the office, so she went to Farmers & Mechanics Bank with a check written by McGinnis and withdrew a thousand. Some of the bills were new. She didn't particularly notice that. The connection is clear. Once we saw we had her dead to rights, she didn't even deny it anymore."

"But what did she say about *why* they wanted to burn Miss Mason's apartment?"

"The reason we supposed. McGinnis bought the original documents from Laura Mason but knew she would keep copies. He wanted to burn the copies. The truth is, Howard McGinnis is a cheap, crude criminal."

"I suppose so, but how do we link him to the murder of Senator Gibson?"

"Ma'am, when I brought that question up, Frieda Schneider broke down in tears and literally beat her head against the table—until I stopped her. She shrieked and wailed and insisted she knew nothing about the murder of Senator Gibson."

"A performance that convinced you, Captain Kennelly?"

"I have to think about it, ma'am. She has confessed everything about the insurance frauds Congressman McGinnis was involved in. She seems resigned to going to prison for her part in that. I—"

"We may have pursued a useful tangential investigation," said the First Lady. "Could it be, Captain, that we caught in our net a big fish that's not the one we were fishing for?"

"It sometimes happens," said Kennelly.

"Well, I congratulate you on it," she said. "And it may not be just tangential, in the end. Do you know where Miss Mason is?"

"I suppose we can find her."

"Accepting money for taking documents from an official file is reason enough to arrest her if she doesn't want to cooperate, is it not?" asked Mrs. Roosevelt.

"Oh, absolutely."

"Let's make sure she is available if we want to ask her further questions," said the First Lady.

"A few hours in one of our cells may make her more truthful than she has been," said Kennelly.

"When might we have results from the laboratory examination of the bloodstained dresses?"

"Shortly, I'm hoping," said Kennelly.

"I'm most interested in that," said Mrs. Roosevelt.

Jerry Baines walked into a handsome little inn on Annandale Road. He had not imagined there would be more than one little bed-and-breakfast on that stretch of road, but in fact this was the third one he had visited.

"Yes, I am Mrs. Barrington. I own and operate the inn. And you are—*Secret Service!*"

Baines tried to reassure her with a disarming smile, but the rail-thin woman behind the desk was not easily reassured. "I would appreciate it if you would just look at a photograph," he said. "Will you, please?"

The woman, reminiscent of the farm wife in Grant Wood's

American Gothic, stared at the picture. "Senator Gibson!" she gasped. "He was murdered!"

"He was a guest here from time to time, if I'm not mistaken," said Baines.

"He . . . Well, yes, as a matter of fact he was."

"And in other circumstances—that is, if he had not been murdered—I would not be asking this question," said Baines. "He did not come alone, and he did not stay overnight. Correct?"

"If he had not been a senator, I would not have—"

"Of course not. I understand. You run a respectable establishment. I am not here to suggest otherwise. On the other hand, I am investigating a murder."

Mrs. Barrington came out from behind her desk and gestured toward oaken chairs and a table in front of a cold fieldstone fireplace. "The woman who came here with him— Frankly, I am surprised you did not come to ask about her before."

"She—?"

"I would not have allowed a woman like that to visit here . . . in other circumstances—that is, except in the circumstance that she was with a United States senator."

"A bit more specific, please," said Baines. "Incidentally, this *is* the woman we're talking about?" He handed her a photograph of Constance Harrison that had been taken the night when Senator Gibson was killed. The guests had been photographed for a souvenir album of the dinner. "This woman?"

"Yes. Not the kind of woman I would allow to occupy a room here," said Mrs. Barrington.

"Specifically . . . ?"

"She was a *prostitute,* Mr. Baines. I have no doubt of it. A prostitute."

Baines looked at the Constance Harrison in the photograph he had shown this woman: a woman dressed for a dinner at the White House, a woman with unusual presence and dignity, in his experience. "I have to ask what makes you think she was a prostitute, Mrs. Barrington."

"Mr. Baines, there are standards of conduct followed by honest women. She— This is embarrassing to say. In the first place, they only came during the day, never to stay overnight, never to eat a meal. When they were checking in, this woman would stand with her arm around his waist, *rubbing her hip against his!* Laughing! Mr. Baines, I do not listen at the doors of my guest rooms. But I didn't have to, to hear this woman crying out in . . . Well, in ecstasy. And then—I hire only one maid, Mr. Baines, a colored woman who has been with me thirty years. One afternoon she came downstairs— Can a Negro woman turn pale? I suppose not. But in the hall she had encountered Senator Gibson's woman, trotting down the hall to the bathroom. Indecently— Wearing a black garter belt and stockings, Mr. Baines! Nothing more! If he had not been a senator . . ."

"I understand, Mrs. Barrington," said Baines. "But let me ask you—when were they here last?"

"Knowing he was murdered on the fifth of June, I checked my register," she said. "They had been here the afternoon before. And that was an occasion!"

"An occasion? In what respect?"

"Yelling and screaming! I mean, on her part. She seems to have gone hysterical. I resolved that afternoon that I would not register them again, senator or no senator."

"Could you overhear anything they said?"

"No. I was down here. But I could hear her shrieking! I— Oh, my God! Do you suppose *she* killed him? Is that why you've come? She's the type who *could.* She's a *whore,* Mr. Baines! That woman is a *whore!* I don't allow women like that in my inn. I'm a widow, Mr. Baines, trying to run a respectable little business! I don't 'low women like that in my rooms!"

* * *

Louis Overmeyer shook his head at Ed Kennelly. "You don't come around with easy ones, do you, Ed? This blood is a week old and—"

"I know," said Kennelly. "But what've you got?"

The lab technician grimaced. " 'What've you got?' 'What've you got?' Like I could get blood out of a turnip."

"So, if you've got anything, you're a genius, Louie. If I hadn't known you're a genius, I wouldn't have brought the sample to you; I'd have taken it to some other genius."

"So long as we understand," said the technician. "Okay. There's only one blood type here. I cut snips from a lot of points on the fabric. These two women stained their dresses on one person's blood, not two or three. Alcohol, point-oh-seven percent. Not drunk. Creatinine high, meaning he drank a lot but was not drunk when he died. Dry-cleaning fluid. Okay, that's from the fabric, not something he'd swallowed. Fabric sizing, same thing. And then what I figure you're looking for. Just a trace. Just a trace but definitely present. I repeated the test six times, with samples from different snips of the fabric. Chloral hydrate. A weak dose. Not enough to knock him out. Enough to make him wanta take a quick nap. If I wanted to slip the guy a Mickey, I'd have dosed him with a lot more than he got."

"You're saying that when the Senator died he was—"

The lab technician made a sign with both hands: like a boat rocking. "Woozy," he said.

Mrs. Roosevelt read a telegram from the office of the county coroner, Ada County, Idaho—

CHARLES GIBSON FATHER OF SENATOR ALSO MARY GIBSON HIS MOTHER LIE BURIED IN CENTRAL CEMETERY BOISE STOP CHARLES SENIOR GRANDFATHER AND DOROTHY HIS WIFE GRANDMOTHER IN SAME CEMETERY STOP HALE SCOTTY MCCABE BURIED IN SILVER CITY CEMETERY OWYHEE COUNTY STOP NO

RECORD HERE OF BIRTH DEATH OF MOTHER AMELIA MCCABE
GIBSON STOP NO RECORD OF CREMATION OF ANY MEMBER OF
EITHER FAMILY STOP NO CREMATORIUM HERE STOP

Another telegram had arrived from the office of the editor
of the Boise *Advertiser*. It read—

FOLLOWING SENT ONLY ON YOUR ASSURANCE INFORMATION IS
ESSENTIAL TO INVESTIGATION MURDER OF SENATOR GIBSON
STOP INFORMATION INCLUDES RUMORS STOP TAKE NOTE OF YOUR
ASSURANCE DISCRETION WILL BE USED IN RELEASING INFORMA-
TION STOP MOTHER OF AMELIA MCCABE GIBSON UNDERSTOOD TO
HAVE BEEN PROSTITUTE IN SILVER CITY DISORDERLY HOUSE
SUBSEQUENTLY MADAM OF SAME STOP HALE SCOTTY MCCABE
REPUTEDLY OWNER OF HOUSE STOP MCCABE NONETHELESS
HIGHLY RESPECTED CITIZEN AND ONE OF WEALTHIEST IN STATE
STOP VANCE GIBSON WELL RESPECTED LAWYER STOP MUCH
CONCERN HERE THAT REPUTATIONS WILL BE DAMAGED STOP
GIBSON WOULD HAVE WON REELECTION EASILY STOP PLEASE
GIVE US A CHANCE TO REVIEW INFORMATION BEFORE GENERAL
RELEASE STOP WE FEEL WE KNOW THESE PEOPLE BETTER THAN
WASHINGTON DOES STOP

Ed Kennelly sat down again in the apartment shared by
Brenda Frelinghuysen and Joanne Winthrop.

"I'm satisfied," he said, "that Joanne Winthrop didn't
murder Senator Gibson."

"Though she might have had motive," said Brenda Frelinghuysen.

He nodded. "Yes, she might have had motive. Let me
characterize you two young women. Correct me where you
find me wrong. You are what are called debs—debutantes.
In life . . . What you do in life— You are ornaments. Oh, I
don't condemn you, Miss Frelinghuysen. But isn't that what
you are, you and Miss Winthrop?"

"I might express the matter in different words, Captain,

but I won't disagree. Neither of us had any choice, you know. That's what Joanne and I were reared to be."

"I'm not scornful," said Kennelly.

"Thank you, Captain. Many people don't understand."

Brenda Frelinghuysen was not today dressed in hostess pajamas. Even so, her costume intrigued Kennelly. She wore a pale blue light cotton sweater and cotton-knit slacks.

"Is Miss Winthrop leaving for Boston soon?" he asked.

"She's said nothing to me about it."

"She indicated she couldn't afford to live in Washington anymore."

Brenda Frelinghuysen shrugged. "She's having lunch at DuPont's—and paying for her own, I think. She's shown no sign of running out of money."

"Can I find her there?"

"Lunch at twelve-thirty, I believe."

"Senator, it's good of you to take my call," said Mrs. Roosevelt.

"Not at all," said Claude Pepper, the Senator from Florida. "What can I do for you, dear lady?"

"I would like to talk to you about last Wednesday evening," she said. "Then I'd like to ask if you might be available for a meeting I may be able to arrange this evening."

"Ma'am," said Pepper, "I am available to you any time you wish."

"My dear," said Mrs. Roosevelt to Amelia Gibson, "we may be able to close the investigation into Senator Gibson's murder. I mean this evening. Often I have called people to meet in the Cabinet Room when I felt we could achieve something important by getting a group together and bringing a mystery to a conclusion. I wonder if in this case we might not sit down on your terrace?"

"We can sit down on the back porch of hell, Mrs. Roosevelt, if it will help to identify the man or woman who killed my husband."

"Shall we say six this evening? I think I can assemble the principals then."

"Of course," said Amelia Gibson. "May I hope the occasion will not be so grim that I shouldn't set out a buffet and a bar?"

"As you wish," said the First Lady.

"Mrs. Roosevelt . . . Do you think you may know who killed Vance?"

"I am all but certain of it, my dear. I am all but certain."

XIII

They met at 6:30 on the stone terrace behind the manor house. The sky was cloudless, the sun still shone brightly, and the Blue Ridge Mountains were visible in the distance.

Amelia Gibson had been riding and had not changed out of her boots and jodhpurs, which she wore with a short-sleeve white silk blouse and a black velvet cap. She had tossed her riding crop on one of the tables, and when Mrs. Roosevelt arrived she was busy directing the household staff about setting up the buffet and bar.

"I am so pleased to see you again, Mrs. Roosevelt," she said. "And Senator Pepper, too. Senator, have you come to help with the investigation?"

"I may have a fact or two that will contribute," said Pepper.

The next car that arrived was driven by Ed Kennelly. Jerry Baines was with him in the front seat. In the back, handcuffed together, were Laura Mason and Frieda Schneider, dressed in the gray cotton uniforms of the D.C. jail. When they walked out onto the terrace, linked together by their wrists, they were obviously in shock and close to tears.

"Laura, for God's sake!" cried Amelia. "Why?"

Laura Mason could not say why. She couldn't find her voice.

Mrs. Roosevelt quietly suggested to Kennelly that he take the handcuffs off.

Kennelly winked. "A little of the *trappings* of the system sometimes loosens tongues," he said. He unlocked the handcuffs. Both women sank into chairs and said nothing.

Joanne Winthrop arrived next, accompanied by Brenda Frelinghuysen. Miss Frelinghuysen had borrowed a car and had driven out from Washington. They were dressed in summer frocks: Joanne's pink, Brenda's butter yellow.

Amelia introduced herself to them, then introduced Mrs. Roosevelt and Senator Pepper—not knowing that the First Lady had already met Joanne. She frowned and said, "This is Laura Mason, who worked in my husband's office. And I don't know who *she* is."

"Her name is Frieda Schneider. She works for Congressman McGinnis," said Mrs. Roosevelt.

Finally, Constance Harrison arrived. She strode out on to the terrace, dressed in white and wearing a white straw hat with a floppy wide brim. "Amelia! What in the world is this? What sort of affair are you having here. And . . . *Mrs. Roosevelt!* What? And why?"

"All will be made plain shortly," said Mrs. Roosevelt.

"This is one of those . . . meetings, like in a mystery play or movie," said Amelia. "We are going to find out who murdered my husband. Perhaps everyone should have a drink first, and something to eat." She snapped her finger at the black man behind the bar, and he poured her a double shot of bourbon, over ice. "Mrs. Roosevelt? What will you have?"

Everyone gathered around the tables and took plates of hors d'oeuvres, then took drinks—everyone but Frieda Schneider and Laura Mason, who only sat in silence, Frieda staring at her hands in her lap. Kennelly brought them two plates of food, and Laura nodded acquiescence to his suggestion that he bring them two whiskies.

"Well," said Amelia when all were again seated. "Who did it? We have here the chief of the homicide squad of the D.C. police, also a senior agent of the Secret Service. And, as I understand, Mrs. Roosevelt has taken a personal interest in the investigation—for which I am grateful. How do we begin?"

Mrs. Roosevelt glanced at Kennelly, then said, "It may, I think, be useful to explain who Miss Schneider is. Or—" She turned to Frieda Schneider. "Maybe you would rather explain that yourself."

The woman looked up at last, with an expression of anguish and apprehension. "I am an administrative assistant to Representative Howard McGinnis. Before he came to Washington, I sold insurance out of his office in Columbus, Ohio."

"Let's be a little more exact about what you did in Columbus," said Kennelly. "You didn't really *sell* insurance. Did you?"

Frieda Schneider sighed. "We didn't have to. We were politically connected and used the insurance business as a front."

"A front for taking graft from Ohio businesses," said Kennelly. "You were the bag woman. You collected the money, and you made the payoffs."

"Everyone trusted me," she said quietly.

"Sometimes you carried the money that paid criminals for things like arson."

"Please . . . What do you want from me? I'm going to prison. Isn't it enough?"

"Maybe you don't have to go to the reformatory," said Kennelly. "If you help us identify the murderer of Senator Gibson."

Frieda Schneider began to weep. "If telling you Howard McGinnis killed Senator Gibson would get me out of this horrible mess, I'd tell you that," she sobbed. "But I don't know he did. I don't have any evidence that he did."

"Why did he want to torch the apartment building on West Virginia Avenue burned?"

"I confessed to that. He wanted to destroy the copies he supposed Miss Mason had made, of the Mayo letters."

"Let me understand something directly," said Mrs. Roosevelt. "Do you say that Congressman McGinnis gave you a direct order to carry money and instructions to Mr. Gordon to hire an arsonist and secure the burning of that building?"

"I have signed a written statement saying that."

"The district attorney has her statement—plus Jack Gordon's and Rudy Ballou's," said Kennelly.

"Then I think we must turn to another point," said the First Lady. "There are several women here who were in love with Senator Gibson. At least one—and I suspect more than one—were sincerely in love with him."

"I was in love with my husband," said Amelia. "And he was in love with me. I can assure you of that."

"But he was intimate with others, was he not?" asked Mrs. Roosevelt.

Amelia lifted her chin, and her face hardened. "I have no doubt," she said.

"Miss Mason," said Mrs. Roosevelt. "Will you tell Mrs. Gibson why you are in jail?"

Laura Mason stared for a moment at Amelia Gibson, then said, "I was desperately in need of money. With the Senator gone, I no longer had a job. I needed something to live on until I could take the bar examination. So I lifted some papers from the office files and sold them to Congressman McGinnis. Those were the Mayo letters that Frieda just mentioned. I thought I—" She turned her eyes on Kennelly. "I thought I wasn't going to be arrested, since I'd told the truth."

Laura Mason looked down at her gray uniform dress and—only half consciously perhaps—ran her hands over it to smooth the wrinkles. She glanced around for sympathy in her humiliation, and found it in the face of the First Lady. She sobbed.

"Were you in love with the Senator?" asked Mrs. Roosevelt.

"It makes me sound cheap to say I wasn't," said Laura. "But I—"

"What makes you sound cheap?" Amelia demanded.

Laura looked at Amelia. "I slept with him," she said simply. "But I was realistic. I knew he didn't love me. I was just an employee who was conveniently available."

"*When* did you do this?" Constance Harrison demanded. "And *where?*"

"For a long time," said Laura. "In his apartment, in Georgetown."

"That was why he was obsessive about having the place thoroughly cleaned every morning by a maid," said Kennelly. "He didn't want any woman to know another had been there."

Mrs. Roosevelt noticed that Joanne Winthrop had blanched.

"When was the *last time* you . . . slept with him?" asked Constance Harrison.

Laura Mason turned cold eyes on the white-hatted Constance Harrison. "The fact is," she said, "I never *slept* with him. He didn't go to sleep when he was in bed with *me*. And the last time?" She shrugged. "A month ago. About."

Constance Harrison so tightened her lips that they turned white. "Cheap . . ." she muttered.

"Why? Did he go to sleep on you?"

"Cheap," Constance Harrison repeated.

"Before that word is bandied around much more," said Baines, "I suggest we obtain the testimony of a Mrs. Barrington who keeps a bed-and-breakfast inn on Annandale Road. She is distinctly of the impression that the Senator brought a prostitute there one or two afternoons a week.

She told me she would not have allowed Mr. Gibson and his prostitute to check into her inn again, no matter if he *was* a United States Senator. She complains of screaming and fighting—and of the woman running through the halls in her underwear."

"It sounds to me like a case of mistaken identity," said Brenda Frelinghuysen.

Amelia sighed. She beckoned to the house man to bring her another drink, though she had ample whiskey left in the glass she had. "It's the penalty a woman pays for being short and dumpy and marrying a tall, handsome man," she said. "I knew he played around. I was always confident, though, that he loved me. He never stopped telling me he did."

"How much money did the Senator give you, Miss Mason?" asked Mrs. Roosevelt.

"Twenty dollars here, twenty dollars there," said Laura Mason. "The total didn't come to three hundred."

"I've been wondering what motive you could possibly have had for wanting the Senator dead," said Mrs. Roosevelt. "Apart from that, I can't see your opportunity."

"I didn't kill him, and I don't know who did," said Laura Mason flatly. "His death is just about the worst thing that ever happened to me."

"The worst thing that ever happened to me, too," murmured Frieda Schneider.

Amelia Gibson shoved a small sandwich into her mouth. "If you have eliminated two suspects," she said, "then just where is this discussion leading? Or are all the suspects here?"

"It becomes more painful," said Mrs. Roosevelt. "Mr. Baines—"

Baines put aside his plate and his glass. "I am sorry to have to embarrass you, Mrs. Harrison," he said, "but the woman Mrs. Barrington thought was a prostitute, the shrieking woman who ran through the halls of her inn in less than a complete set of underwear, was you."

"How dare you."

"She identified you from your photograph. So did her maid."

"Connie! For Christ's sake! You too?" shrilled Amelia.

Constance Harrison lifted her chin and cast a scornful gaze on Amelia. "There was a very great difference," she said. "Vance was in love with me. He— This Mrs. Barrington . . . How dare she say what you tell me she said."

"Suggest a reason why she would lie," said Kennelly.

"How would I know why she would lie?"

"For some time . . ." said Baines. "What—two or three years?—you and Senator Gibson had been paying afternoon visits to Mrs. Barrington's little inn. I'm sorry to have to betray your confidence, but you told me you did. This Mrs. Barrington told me you conducted yourself like—"

"Like a slut!" yelled Amelia. "How *could* you? You were my guest here. You called yourself my friend."

"I was never your friend, Amelia. I was *his* friend. He and I were deeply and sincerely—yes, even innocently—in love, the way you and he never were, never could be."

"On Tuesday afternoon," said Baines calmly. "That is, Tuesday before last, the day before the Senator died, you and he had a loud fight in your room at the inn. Mrs. Barrington describes it as hysterical."

"A lovers' quarrel . . ."

"About what?" asked Mrs. Roosevelt.

"I don't even remember . . ."

"Then let me refresh your recollection," said the First Lady. "The Senator told you that afternoon that he was not going to see you anymore. He told you he was in love with a younger woman. Didn't he?"

"So I killed him, then?" asked Constance Harrison dully.

"I don't know yet," said Mrs. Roosevelt. "I don't know as

a matter of certainty that is what he told you. But it was, wasn't it?"

Constance Harrison nodded.

"Another one!" cried Amelia Gibson.

"The love of his life," said Mrs. Roosevelt, unable to keep a trace of cynicism out of her voice. "If he was capable of having one." She glanced around the terrace. "Who was she? Who was the love of his life?"

Joanne Winthrop had begun to sob loudly. Her face had turned red, and she covered it with her hands and shook with sobs. Brenda Frelinghuysen stood and bent over her, trying to comfort her.

"It is true, isn't it, Mrs. Harrison?" asked the First Lady quietly. "On Tuesday afternoon, in the inn on Annandale Road, he said good-bye to you. You became hysterical. Most women would, I suppose. You had violated your own marriage vows and encouraged him to violate his. To— Well, I suppose to protect his career, you had sneaked about, surrendered every element of your dignity, seized every little opportunity to be with him, and made the most of every one of them. You made yourself a—"

"To keep his interest, I made myself into the image Mrs. Barrington saw," said Constance Harrison bitterly.

"Now he told you he was going to abandon his wife and home, and his seat in the Senate, and run away with a young woman."

"Even so, I didn't kill him," she whispered.

"No, I don't suppose you did," said Mrs. Roosevelt. "But maybe you made it possible for someone else to do it. Of that we aren't sure. Not yet."

Brenda Frelinghuysen walked over to Kennelly and confronted him angrily. "You gave me your unqualified assurance that you did not think of Joanne as a suspect."

"Even if I did, if she is, she is," said Kennelly.

"Miss Winthrop is not here as a suspect, Miss Frelinghuysen," said the First Lady. "She is here because she possesses certain facts we need to conclude this investigation. Are you prepared to talk with us, Miss Winthrop?"

Joanne Winthrop nodded. "I've already told you most of what there is to tell," she said.

"Told who?" asked Amelia.

"She told me," said Mrs. Roosevelt. "Go on, Miss Winthrop."

Joanne glanced around, at the faces of the people around her: finding sympathy in the faces of the First Lady and Brenda Frelinghuysen, and expressions from curiosity to hostility in the others. "Vance loved me," she said simply and with dignity. "I suppose he loved his wife once. I don't know if he loved Mrs. Harrison. I didn't know anything about Miss Mason—except I knew he was a lusty man who probably sowed his wild oats. That made no difference to me. From the day I met him, I knew—"

"Slut . . ." muttered Amelia.

Joanne glanced at Amelia Gibson, her expression a mixture of pity and scorn—but with no hostility. "I am a debutante of the Silver Rose. I made my debut in Vienna. That was what he wanted: a woman he could be proud of. Sooner or later he would have arranged the divorce. He wasn't sure how, but he would have arranged it, and we would have been married."

"And in the meantime he looted my inheritance to get the money you two would need to live well," said Amelia caustically.

"You had a joint estate," said Joanne. "Half of it was his. He wouldn't have taken more than half."

"The afternoon before he died, he gave you fifty thousand dollars in cash," said Mrs. Roosevelt. "Didn't he?"

"Yes, he did."

"Ha!" mocked Amelia. "The afternoon before he told Connie to get out of his life. Did you get any money, Connie? If you didn't, you weren't as smart as this one. She got fifty thousand. That's a record. I've known him to pay ten."

"She's pregnant," said Constance Harrison scornfully. "That's why she got fifty thousand: to rear the child."

Once more, Joanne Winthrop clutched her face in both hands and moaned in anguish.

"She is not pregnant," said Mrs. Roosevelt. "The shock of learning of the Senator's death caused a miscarriage."

Brenda Frelinghuysen glanced sharply at the First Lady. Then her face softened, and she said, "That's right. Joanne lives with me, and the news of the Senator's murder all but killed her."

" 'News,' " Amelia sneered. "She was looking for a way to kill him, came to the White House and somehow got in, and—"

"How could she have known," asked Mrs. Roosevelt, "that Senator Gibson would leave his table in the middle of a state dinner, and go to the East Room?"

Amelia shot an angry glance at Constance Harrison. *"She* knew. She went out about the same time."

"Twice, in fact," said Mrs. Roosevelt. "You went out some fifteen minutes earlier, Mrs. Harrison, then again when the Senator did. You explained of the second time that you and the Senator had promised to meet in the East Room for a quick but intimate kiss. In view of what we've heard, I hardly think he would have agreed to meet you."

Constance Harrison's brittle composure had softened, and suddenly she looked twenty years older. She put her straw hat aside, as if it were now too happy. "I went out to beg him not to leave me," she said.

"And what about the first time when you went out?"

"I had signaled him. I misinterpreted his reaction. I thought he had nodded an indication he would come outside and talk with me. I went out and stood around like a fool. He did not come out."

"A woman could not have killed him," murmured Joanne sadly. "He was a big, strong man. To cut his throat with a razor . . ." She shook her head.

"So we had assumed," said Mrs. Roosevelt. "So we had assumed."

"So who does that leave?" asked Amelia. "You don't have any men suspects here. Was it Howard McGinnis?"

"I would like to ask you a question, Amelia," said the First Lady. "You had the Senator's body cremated. You scattered the ashes in Bull Run, and you threw the urn in after them. That being the case, it became impossible to have an autopsy."

"Wasn't there an autopsy?" asked Amelia.

"No. It was a mistake. There should have been. But the cause of death was so obvious that it wasn't done. Then cremation made it impossible. If it were possible, we would have the body exhumed for an autopsy."

"Whatever it would have proved is lost now," said Amelia glumly. "I expected better."

"Was cremation common in his family?" asked Mrs. Roosevelt.

Amelia shrugged. "I don't know. It was what he wanted."

"Actually," said Mrs. Roosevelt, "no one of his family was ever cremated before. No one of your family ever was. This was unique."

"So?"

"Well . . . If there had been an autopsy, chloral hydrate would have been found in the Senator's blood. A poison. Sometimes called knockout drops. Sometimes called a 'Mickey Finn.' When Senator Gibson left the table, he said he was ill. And indeed he was. He had been dosed with chloral hydrate."

"Who says so?" Amelia asked. "How can you know, if there was no autopsy."

"Our dresses," said Mrs. Roosevelt. "Yours and mine. They were soaked with his blood—enough blood for the police laboratory to analyze and find the chloral hydrate."

"How could that be?" asked Amelia. "Who could possibly have given it to him?"

"Let's start with something," said Kennelly. "It had to be given by someone who know how much to use. Too much, he'd have fallen on his face. Too little, he'd still have been strong enough to fight back when someone came at him to cut his throat. Now, where in the world could a person have gotten that knowledge? That's knowledge gained from experience."

"Well, who has that kind of experience?" Amelia demanded testily.

"Dear . . ." said Mrs. Roosevelt softly. "Who does have?"

"All right, who? Who do you think?"

Kennelly spoke. "Someone who spent most of a lifetime in a business where knockout drops were commonly used," he said.

"Amelia . . ." said Mrs. Roosevelt. "I don't want to humiliate you. You have troubles enough. But do you want to answer the question? Who is the lady dressed in white, who rides a horse here at Fairlea? I've seen her twice. Mrs. Harrison saw and heard her one night. I believe I know who she is. Do you want to tell us?"

"That is none of your business," said Amelia. "I don't mean to be rude, but it really is none of your business and has nothing to do with what we're talking about."

"I can go upstairs and ask the lady who she is," said Kennelly.

"You are not a policeman here, Captain Kennelly," said Amelia coldly.

"Then I'll tell you who she is without asking her," said Kennelly. "She's your mother. She once worked in a bawdy house in Silver City, Idaho. Later, she was the proprietor. She would have known how to use knockout drops. That was wild territory thirty and forty years ago. They used knockout drops to quiet boisterous drunks and settle threatening bullies—to put the best face on it. They used knockout drops to rob men, too. Even if your mother never used them, she'd have known how. She'd have known the dosage."

Amelia Gibson stared at the First Lady. "Am I to understand you are about to accuse *me* of murdering my husband?" she asked.

"You had ample motive," said Mrs. Roosevelt.

"And how am I supposed to have slipped knockout drops into Vance's glass? I was seated *across* the table from him."

"Who was seated next to you?" asked Mrs. Roosevelt.

"Senator Pepper."

The First Lady nodded at the Senator from Florida. "I believe you can furnish the last clue that solves the mystery, Senator," she said.

Senator Pepper nodded gravely. "Miz Gibson," he said, "after we'd drunk a toast and had sat down again, you leaned across the table with your wine glass and offered to interlock arms with your husband, so he could take a sip from your glass and he could take a sip from yours. That was a playful gesture, and you did it with a big smile. He drank from your glass, Miz Gibson." The Senator nodded. "He drank from your glass."

Amelia Gibson glared at the Senator, then at the First Lady. Pale and furious, she said nothing.

"You waited a minute or so," said Mrs. Roosevelt, "then went out, knowing you'd find him somewhere, either collapsed or on the verge of collapse. Either would suit your purpose, so long as you could find him alone. He had gone in the East Room and sat down on a chair near the door, trying to recover his equilibrium."

"I can testify to that," said Constance Harrison. "I left him in the East Room. I'd wanted to talk to him, to beg him to change his mind about what he'd told me at the inn the afternoon before; but he was obviously ill. He asked me to leave him alone, and I did. If I had stayed beside him—" She sobbed deeply and dropped her chin to her chest.

"You found him sitting there," said Mrs. Roosevelt to

Amelia. "He was only half conscious. And he was alone. You stepped behind him and put one arm around him, as if to embrace him. Then with the razor you'd taken out of your handbag, you cut his throat."

Amelia shrugged.

"You walked over to the piano and dropped the razor inside. You knew it would be found sooner or later, but it wouldn't be found on you. On the way back to your husband you realized your skirt had dragged through his blood and was soaked with it. You saw also your gloves were stained with blood. You knelt beside him and soaked up even more blood, in the expectation that people who found you kneeling in his blood and embracing his bloody body would accept that as the explanation for your dress and gloves being bloody. Then you screamed."

"When I swam in the grotto Tuesday—"

"Mrs. Roosevelt!" Kennelly exclaimed. "You swam—"

"Never mind. Amelia told me that afternoon that her husband had been withdrawing large amounts of money from their joint accounts. I thought at the time it was a strange thing for her to tell me, since obviously it gave her a motive for wanting him dead. I realized on reflection that she was only telling me something she knew we'd find out sooner or later."

"In other words, she was covering herself," said Baines.

"I imagine she needed to," said Kennelly with a sly smile.

"Captain—"

Two officers of the Virginia state police had taken Amelia Gibson away. Kennelly had called them, and they had extended full cooperation. No one remained on the terrace now but Mrs. Roosevelt, Kennelly and Baines, Laura Mason and Frieda Schneider—now once more handcuffed together—and Senator Pepper, he because he had come in the White House car.

The old woman in white appeared for a moment at a window above the terrace. She stuck out her tongue at the people below, then disappeared.

Senator Claude Pepper shook his head and smiled. "My dear lady," he said to Mrs. Roosevelt, "I've always heard you lead an interestin' and adventuresome life, but I hadn't imagined! I thank you for lettin' me make my little contribution in person. Why, I wouldn't have missed this evenin' for the *world!*"

EPILOGUE

Amelia McCabe Gibson was convicted of the murder of Senator Vance Gibson and sentenced to life imprisonment. She entered the federal reformatory for women at Alderson, West Virginia, on September 3, 1940. On September 5, 1960, she was released on parole. At the time of her release she was fifty-five years old, and since she had been unable to spend money for twenty years, she was far wealthier in 1960 than she had been in 1940. What was more, since she had been unable for twenty years to indulge her tastes in food and drink, she was twenty pounds lighter.

Her mother, who was seventy-five, still lived at Fairlea, which had been administered during Amelia's term of imprisonment by an Alexandria bank as trustee. Amelia moved back into the house and lived there until her mother died in February, 1964. She then sold the estate and bought an elegant mansion on Massachusetts Avenue NW— Embassy Row.

There she entertained an eclectic crowd and won a new circle of friends. Conservative Washington society professed amazement that diplomats, congressmen, and even officers of the Cabinet would accept the invitations of a

198

woman who had murdered her husband by slitting his throat with a razor. She was, though, a subject of curiosity, and during her years of confinement she had developed a new and quiet charm—mostly by having been subdued. She was invited, as well as giving invitations, and soon was a familiar figure at cocktail parties and dinners.

The city had another surprise in store. In December, 1964 she married Captain Paul Jarring, a Swedish naval officer she had met at a reception at the Swedish embassy. He was of a distinguished family, with a mansion in Stockholm and a country estate on a lake. They divided their time among three homes. In the fall of 1965 a naughty *paparazzo* using a long telephoto lens photographed Amelia Jarring romping naked in the snow outside the family sauna, switching herself with willow twigs.

She outlived Captain Jarring, too, and today lives quietly and obscurely in a retirement village in Palm Beach.

Joanne Winthrop kept the fifty thousand dollars Vance Gibson had given her the day before he died. Indeed, Amelia Gibson never asked for its return. Joanne remained in Washington. In 1942 she was commissioned a captain in the Women's Army Corps. During a period of service in England, she met Brigadier Sir William Buttersfield, Lord Willingham. They were married in 1944, at which time she surrendered her commission in the W.A.C. and her American citizenship, becoming a British subject. When the Earl of Willingham died in 1947, her husband inherited the title. Joanne, Countess Willingham, survived her husband, who died in 1984. She divides her time between her flat in Mayfair and her villa at St. Tropez. Her opinions of pre-Raphaelite art are widely sought. She has published more than forty articles on the subject.

Laura Mason was released from the D.C. jail the day after the meeting on the terrace at Fairlea. Charges against her were dropped. She passed the bar examination and was admitted to the District bar. She practiced law from 1940 until 1962, when she was appointed a judge of the United States District Court by President Kennedy. She retired in 1983 and died in 1987.

Frieda Schneider was allowed to plead guilty to the charge of arson alone and was sentenced to ten years. She was confined in the same reformatory as Amelia Gibson for five-and-a-half years, then was released and returned to Columbus, Ohio, where she was appointed to a clerkship in the office of the county auditor. Subsequently she worked as an administrative assistant in the office of the state auditor. She retired in 1973 and died in 1988.

Congressman Howard McGinnis spent twelve years in prison. He went home to Columbus and was appointed deputy to the state insurance commissioner. When Democratic Governor Frank Lausche replaced Republican Governor John Bricker, McGinnis was dismissed. He was appointed assistant clerk of the probate court but died of a heart attack before he could assume his new duties.

Jack "Flash" Gordon spent six years in a federal prison, for arson. His wife kept his insurance agency going until his release, and he remained an insurance agent until his death in 1979.

Rudolph "Rudy" Ballou spent six years in a federal prison. He disappeared after that, presumably taking a new identity.

Constance Harrison's name was not associated with the murder of Senator Gibson. She survived her husband by fifteen years and died in 1976.

Through the influence of Mrs. Roosevelt and Joanne Winthrop, Lena Madison secured a job as assistant to the housekeeper of The Willows, the women's apartment hotel where Joanne had lived before she moved in with Brenda Frelinghuysen. Lena Madison ultimately became the housekeeper of the hotel, but had to leave when it was torn down in 1970. By then she was a recognized leader of the N.A.A.C.P. and was appointed an organizer. She retired in 1991.

*   *   *

Three days after the meeting on the Fairlea terrace, Winston Churchill made his "finest hour" speech. Three days after that, President Roosevelt appointed Henry Stimson Secretary of War and Frank Knox Secretary of the Navy.

On Saturday, June 22, 1940, France surrendered to Germany.